He couldn't see her at first....

But then he spotted a flash of red near the entrance. The stranger who had stopped her earlier was beside her as they moved quickly toward the door.

"Kendall!"

Whether she somehow heard him over the roar of the panicked crowd, or whether the force of his gaze drew her attention, Graham didn't know. But at that exact moment she glanced back, her gaze clinging to his and he saw her lips move. *I'm sorry.*

Sorry for what? Graham thought a split second before he found himself pushed back against the wall.

He called out to Kendall, but his voice was lost in the din. Frantic to reach her, Graham tore himself free and fought his way through the terrified mob.

But by the time he reached the door, his wife had vanished.

AMANDA STEVENS

TEXAS RANSOM

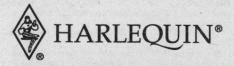

HARLEQUIN®

TORONTO • NEW YORK • LONDON
AMSTERDAM • PARIS • SYDNEY • HAMBURG
STOCKHOLM • ATHENS • TOKYO • MILAN • MADRID
PRAGUE • WARSAW • BUDAPEST • AUCKLAND

ISBN-13: 978-0-373-69302-3
ISBN-10:   0-373-69302-8

TEXAS RANSOM

ABOUT THE AUTHOR

Amanda Stevens is a bestselling author of more than thirty novels of romantic suspense. In addition to being a Romance Writers of America RITA® Award finalist, she is also a recipient of awards for Career Acheivement in Romantic/Mystery and Career Acheivement in Romantic/Suspense from *Romantic Times BOOKreviews*. She currently resides in Texas. To find out more about past, present and future projects, please visit her Web site at www.amandastevens.com.

Books by Amanda Stevens

HARLEQUIN INTRIGUE
759—SILENT STORM*
777—SECRET PASSAGE*
796—UNAUTHORIZED PASSION
825—INTIMATE KNOWLEDGE
844—MATTERS OF SEDUCTION
862—GOING TO EXTREMES
882—THE EDGE OF ETERNITY
930—SECRETS OF HIS OWN
954—DOUBLE LIFE
1035—TEXAS RANSOM

MIRA BOOKS
THE DOLLMAKER

*Quantum Men

CAST OF CHARACTERS

Graham Hollister—When his wife is kidnapped, he uncovers a web of international intrigue, betrayal and a brutal enemy with a terrifying vendetta.

Kendall Hollister—A woman with a shrouded past.

Leo Kittering—A man who will stop at nothing to avenge his dead son.

Gabriel Esteban—He possesses the name of an angel and the soul of a devil.

Hector Reyes—A henchman caught between a rock and a hard place.

Michael Barron—Graham's best friend has a few secrets of his own.

Terrence Hollister—Graham's older brother and bitter rival has a failing business in desperate need of cash.

Prologue

A waxing moon rose over the barren countryside as the black SUV bumped along a back road that ran parallel to the border. Two hundred yards away, across the Rio Grande, was Big Bend National Park, a vast terrain of canyons, desert and mountains. A place where a man could stay invisible for days if he needed to.

Leo Kittering sat alone in the back seat and stared straight ahead as the headlights tunneled through the darkness. He glanced back once, made uneasy by their proximity to the border, but the road was clear. Nothing behind them but a swirl of dust that settled slowly in the moonlight.

Kittering turned away from the window. His heart fluttered as adrenaline rushed through his veins. He hadn't felt this exhilarated in years. And with good reason because soon everything would be in place.

The man and woman…they wouldn't know what hit them.

He didn't want to get ahead of himself, though. There was still a lot to be done. Too many things that could yet go wrong. An operation of this magnitude was a delicate balance of careful planning and guesswork.

A part of him wished that he could be there when it all went down, but his time for that kind of work had come and gone. He was no longer a young man or in the best of health. But even if he had still been in his prime, he wouldn't risk crossing the border. If he was spotted and detained by the authorities, the whole plan would be jeopardized.

Besides he didn't need to see their faces at the exact moment they realized their lives were over. He could take just as much satisfaction in the aftermath.

He shifted his considerable weight in the seat and rolled down the window for a breath of fresh air. The man in the front passenger seat glanced over his shoulder. He had a cell phone to his ear, which he lowered for a moment to ask in an anxious voice, "Leo, you okay?"

The older man grunted, neither confirming nor denying the query.

The vehicle came to a stop, and to his right Leo could see the glitter of moonlight on muddy water. For years, American tourists and Mexican villagers had crossed the river in nearby Boquillas, a loosely enforced class-B port of entry. Leo himself had come over not far from there, but that had been a long time ago. The crossing was officially closed now, although residents of the tiny village continued to go back and forth with their livestock. And often with even more valuable cargo.

Leo's mind churned with memories and emotions and with a sudden unease. "They're not here," he muttered as apprehension fingered down his spine.

"Don't worry, they'll show. There's too much at stake for them not to."

I hope you're right, Kittering thought, his eyes still glued to the water. Because if Gabriel Esteban didn't come soon, somebody would have to pay.

As if reading his mind, Hector Reyes—the man with the cell phone—shot him a worried look. "I made the arrangements myself. They'll show," he said again, as if he, too, needed reassuring.

Kittering closed his eyes for a moment, letting the humid air wash over him. He'd brought L.J. here once, when they'd been on a camping trip in Big Bend. The boy couldn't have been more than seven or eight because they'd still been living in San Antonio at the time. Leo had owned his own business even then, been a well-respected member of the community. Happily married, a settled family man. Then a few risky deals had soured and he'd found it necessary to relocate in something of a hurry to Mexico.

His wife, Nina, had refused to come with him. She'd tried to turn L.J. against him, too, but the foolish woman had learned the hard way that you did not keep a father from his only son.

Nina, God rest her soul, had been dead nearly thirty years, and L.J. was gone now, too. But it gave Leo no comfort to imagine that mother and son were reunited in heaven.

The only thing that gave him any pleasure since his son's murder was the promise of revenge. It had been a long time coming. But now the day of reckoning was almost at hand.

"What about Houston?" he growled. "Our contact there can be trusted? You're certain?"

Hector Reyes turned again, his gaze meeting Leo's in the dark. "He knows the consequences of betrayal. Nothing will go wrong."

"An operation like this…we can't be too careful." Leo sank back into deep thought. He wanted to turn his mind away from the past. He needed to get his head back in the game before the others arrived so that he could be on guard for even the smallest hint of treachery.

Leo had never met Gabriel Esteban, but his violent reputation preceded him. Leo wasn't afraid of very many things or very many men. Not after everything he'd seen and done in his sixty-three years on this earth. But the stories he'd heard about Gabriel Esteban chilled even his blood.

Doing business with an animal like that…

Leo shuddered.

His men were jittery, too, especially Hector, who would accompany Esteban and his crew to Houston.

Leo didn't blame Hector for being nervous. He was in a difficult position. If he refused to go with Esteban, he risked Leo's wrath. And if Esteban turned on him once they were across the border, Hector would wish that he'd never been born. The poor man was caught between the proverbial rock and a hard place.

Leo felt only a slight twinge of guilt over Hector's predicament, even though the younger man had worked for him for years. Hector had started in the organization as a kid, a penniless street urchin who'd turned up at Leo's front gate one day, demanding a job. Leo had admired the boy's bravado and his determination to take care of his family, especially his younger sister, Maria. So Leo had given him the odd job around the estate.

But behind Leo's back, Hector and L.J. had become fast friends, and sometime later Leo discovered that the boy had moved into the house. He'd take a room down the hall from L.J.'s and had never left, even when Leo's son went off to university.

After L.J.'s death, Hector had become Leo's right-hand man, and eventually Maria had moved into the house, too. Leo thought the world of both Hector and Maria, but still he didn't hesitate to send him on this dangerous mission. Because when all was said and done, blood was still thicker than water.

A movement in the dark caught Leo's attention, and his eyes narrowed as he focused on the water. A few yards downstream, a teenage boy crossed the shallow river with a donkey. Leo watched until the boy was out of sight, and then he turned slowly as approaching headlights illuminated the interior of his vehicle.

"That'll be him." Hector glanced nervously over the seat. "Are you sure you want to do this?" he asked in Spanish. "Gabriel Esteban is a very dangerous man. Once you agree to his terms, there'll be no turning back."

The driver, who had spoken very little during the drive, cast a wary glance at first Hector and then Leo.

Leo knew what he was thinking. There would be hell to pay for anyone else who dared challenge Leo's judgment.

Everyone who worked for Leo knew of his temper. His control had a way of snapping when it was least expected over the seemingly most inconsequential incident. Part of that was by nature and part of it by design. Leo enjoyed seeing the men's fear. It kept them on their toes.

He'd been a little too lax with Hector. That was another reason he was sending him across the border with Esteban. Hector had become too complacent. And that could spell trouble very quickly in their business.

"I know what I'm doing," Leo snapped. "Now, leave ᵣ ᵇ of you. I want to speak to Esteban alone."

ᵈ the driver climbed out of the vehicle, bᵤ ᵈᵈn't go far. Leo could hear them muttering in Spanish through his open window.

The headlights on the other vehicle went dead, and all at once the darkness of the countryside seemed to envelope Leo. He felt an unfamiliar tightness in his lungs, as if something heavy was pressing against his chest.

Suddenly he couldn't wait to be home, safely ensconced behind the high stucco walls that protected his home from the prying eyes of the *federales*. In the past five years, since L.J.'s death, he'd rarely ventured outside those walls. Now he remembered why. After nearly three decades, the Mexican landscape still seemed foreign to him.

A few minutes passed before Leo saw a tall, dark shadow emerge from the other vehicle and walk slowly across the dusty road toward the SUV. The approaching stranger said something to Hector and the driver, and then Leo heard a soft laugh before Gabriel Esteban opened the door and slid onto the backseat beside him.

The interior light had been disengaged, but moonlight flooded through the windows and Leo could see the barest hint of a smile still lingering at the corners of Esteban's mouth. His was not a nice smile, more like a vicious smirk. His face was pitted with acne scars and his thick eyebrows rose in points above his dark eyes, giving him a demonic appearance befitting his reputation.

In spite of the physical imperfections, Leo had a feeling that Gabriel Esteban never wanted for female companionship. There was something about him, a perverse charisma that would draw a certain kind of woman like a moth to flame.

Gabriel eyes met Leo's in the moonlight and the unpleasant smile deepened. "Señor Kittering."

The sound of his voice drove an icy chill straight through Leo's heart. He was not a man easily intimidated. He'd operated for too many years on the seamy side of society and had turned a blind eye to the havoc his profession wreaked on innocent lives. He'd arranged the "accident" that had removed his wife from his son's life, and he'd never so much as fingered a rosary in regret.

But now the thought of what Gabriel Esteban would do with Leo's money filled his heart with a black, freezing dread. Leo was surely on the road to hell now. He had been for a long time, but now there was no turning back. For what he and Gabriel Esteban had planned, there would be no forgiveness.

"Señor Esteban." He said the name with the respectful wariness befitting two powerful rivals who suddenly found themselves co-conspirators in a diabolical scheme.

"You have the money?"

Leo reached for the laptop on the seat between them. "Half will be transferred into your account now, the other half when the job is finished. Just as we agreed."

Gabriel Esteban nodded. "Then let's get on with it, shall we?"

It took Leo only a few seconds to transfer the funds to the numbered bank account in the Caymans that had been set up for the operation. Once Esteban was satisfied the transaction had gone through, he glanced up. "Relax, *mi amigo*. In a matter of days, we will both have what we want."

"I'll relax when the woman is safely across the border."

"And the man?"

"Do whatever is necessary to gain his cooperation. Then kill him."

Esteban grinned as he opened the door and climbed out, then briefly turned to say over his shoulder, "I'll be in touch. Have your man ready to leave at a moment's notice."

Leo watched him walk back to the other car. The headlights came on, and the vehicle turned, heading down the road in the direction from which it had come.

The front doors of the SUV opened and Hector and the driver got in. Hector glanced at the laptop on the seat beside Leo.

"It's done then?"

"It's done." Leo drew a long breath, settling into the corner of his seat as his gaze went back to the river.

God help him, it was done.

Chapter One

"It feels a little like heaven up here, doesn't it?"

"Only a little?" Graham Hollister teased as he surveyed the city lights from the rooftop of the PemCo Tower, an eighty-five-story glass-and-granite monolith that was now the tallest skyscraper in the Houston skyline.

The building would soon become the oil company's world headquarters, but for now, tonight, it was the culmination of all Graham's dreams.

When he closed his eyes, he could feel the building sway beneath them, and a wave of dizziness washed over him. He fought it off. He didn't want anything to spoil this night.

He tightened his arms around his wife's slim waist. "Only a *little* like heaven," he mused. "Damn. I must be doing something wrong."

She pulled away and shot him a look over her shoulder. "Will you stop fishing? I told you earlier the earth moved. What more do you want?"

"Tell me again. I'm feeling insecure." His hand trailed down her bare arm. "Or better yet, show me."

She slapped at his hand. "Up here? No way! I'm not an exhibitionist."

"Tell that to Myron." Myron was the stray tabby they'd adopted a few months ago when he'd crawled over the fence one day and caught them skinny-dipping in the pool. He'd gotten quite an eyeful before either of them had noticed him stretched out on one of the loungers.

"Different situation entirely," Kendall said. "And besides, Myron doesn't have a judgmental bone in his body."

"And I do?"

"You're not the one I'm worried about. Getting caught in flagrante delicto by the Mexican ambassador is not my idea of a fun evening."

"No, but I bet it would be his," Graham said as he drew her back against him.

Her shampoo smelled like flowers, but her perfume was something darker, headier. That was Kendall. Always a dichotomy. Insecure, dauntless and perfectly flawed. A woman he found endlessly fascinating, even after seven years of marriage. More like five, though, if you counted the long separation.

But Graham didn't want to think about that tonight. He and Kendall had never been happier, so what did it matter that she'd once left him? He hadn't tried to stop her. The truth of the matter was he'd been relieved when she walked out on their marriage.

That had been a long time ago. Things were different now. *They* were different.

And yet there were times, such as earlier tonight before they'd left the hotel, when Graham sensed that maybe everything between them wasn't as perfect as he wanted to believe. Sometimes, when Kendall didn't know he was around, he'd see a look come over her face. Sad, pensive...lost. Graham tried to chalk it up to her past. She didn't talk much about her family, but he knew she'd had a difficult childhood and a troubled adolescence. He'd never pressed for details. He wasn't keen on airing his dirty laundry, either, but at times, he still felt as if he'd barely scratched the surface of who she really was.

"I love you. You know that, right?"

She turned. Was it his imagination or did her smile seem tentative? Wistful? "I love you, too." She lifted her hand to trace his jawline. "It's going to be okay."

His heart did a funny little somersault against his chest. "What is?"

"Tonight," she said, but there was a slight hesitation before she answered.

He nodded and managed a smile although suddenly his mouth had gone dry. Something was going on with her. Something she didn't feel she could share with him.

"Kendall?"

"Yes?"

"Are you sure the earth moved?"

She punched his shoulder. "Forget it. We're not having a quickie on the rooftop to stroke your ego when there's a whole roomful of people waiting downstairs to tell you how wonderful you are."

"Not the same thing at all."

"Seriously, Graham. I'm so proud of you," she said, her eyes suddenly glistening.

That was another thing that had Graham a little concerned. Kendall had been so emotional these past few days. He had no idea what that was all about, and she didn't seem to want to tell him.

"All right," he said reluctantly. "You've convinced me. I suppose we should go downstairs and at least make an appearance."

She nodded. "I need to freshen up first. My hair must be a mess."

"You look beautiful."

"I never look beautiful," she said with a resigned shrug that always broke his heart.

He resisted the urge to trace one of the scars on her face with his fingertip, but she wouldn't like that. Since the last surgery, the imperfections were barely even visible, but she knew they were there. And even after all this time, she was still a little self-conscious in social situations.

To Graham, though, she would always be beautiful.

She started for the elevator, but he caught her arm and she turned back. "What is it?"

He gazed into her eyes. "Are you happy? With me, I mean."

Her lips trembled and for a moment, he thought she was going to cry. Instead she smiled and lifted herself on her tiptoes to remove his glasses before she kissed him.

"Being with you is like being in heaven," she whispered.

"YOU'RE ONE lucky bastard, Graham. I hope you know that."

Graham nodded as he surveyed the glittering crowd that had assembled to celebrate the post-construction phase of the PemCo Tower. "I'm doing okay."

"Doing okay?" Michael Barron, his best friend since their college days at Rice University, clapped him on the back. "I think most folks would say you're doing a little better than okay. Gorgeous wife. Big house. Your own company. And now this…" His blue eyes twinkled. "You're living the dream, buddy."

"You're not doing so badly yourself," Graham said, his gaze still on the crowd. Where the hell was Kendall? She'd gone to freshen up as soon as they came down from the roof, and he hadn't seen her since. That had been several minutes ago. He didn't know why, but her absence made him uneasy.

Or maybe his apprehension that evening had more to do with the argument he'd had with Terrence that morning. He hadn't told Kendall about their latest disagreement because he knew how much she hated the combative relationship he had with his older brother. Terrence always knew how to push his buttons, and Graham should have known better than to let him get to him. After all this time and all the success he'd achieved, he certainly had no reason to feel intimidated.

But somehow in Terrence's presence, Graham always reverted to the insecure geek who'd grown up in the shadow of his football-star brother.

"Oh, don't get me wrong." Michael deftly plucked a champagne glass from the tray of a passing waiter. "I'm living the good life, too. It's just that my career has taken a few unexpected turns. Not you, though." He took a long sip of his drink. "You've had the same goal since we were roommates in college. You always said you were going to design the tallest, grandest building in Houston, and by damn if you didn't pull it off. I admire your focus, Graham. I really do."

Graham tried not to wince at the accolade. Sometimes he wasn't so sure his dedication was anything to be proud of. Career tunnel-vision had almost cost him his marriage, but ever since he and Kendall had reconciled five years ago, he'd made a promise to her and to himself that their relationship would come first no matter what.

He'd been worried when he first took the PemCo contract that it would put too much stress on their marriage. From inception to completion, the project had consumed nearly two years of his life, requiring endless meetings and arduous hours at the computer drafting version after version of the building until a design was finally accepted by the team.

And then came the politics, the disagreements, the costly delays and untold man hours that were inevitable with such an ambitious project. The tension had only escalated once the alliance between Houston-based PemCo and Pemex, the Mexican state-run petroleum company, became public. One of PemCo's refineries had been firebombed in protest, and the mastermind, a former head of the oil workers' labor union named Joaquin Galindo, had been arrested in Mexico City and sent to prison.

There were times when Graham wondered if the project would ever be completed under such volatile conditions. But through it all, Kendall had been supportive in a way he could never have imagined before the accident. The near-death experience had changed her, softened her, made her reevaluate her priorities just as it had Graham.

He really was a lucky guy, Graham thought, taking a sip of his own champagne. He had everything any man could ever want.

"I just never thought I'd find myself working for your brother," Michael was saying. "Let alone occupying the office that should have been yours. That wasn't my plan when I first passed the bar."

Graham shrugged. "You're a better vice president than I ever would be so it all worked out for the best."

"Maybe. But I still say if your old man had lived, he would have eventually worn you down."

"Not a chance. I've never wanted to do anything but design buildings. Dad would have finally accepted that fact. Besides, there's no way I could work with Terrence. One of us would kill the other."

Michael scowled. "This is none of my business, but we've been friends for a long time so I hope you won't take my advice the wrong way. You need to cut Terrence some slack. The company's going through a rough time, and he's got a lot on his plate. That knock-down-drag-out you two had earlier didn't help."

Graham frowned. "What are you talking about? Hollister Motors has always been financially sound." The company his father founded nearly forty years ago had given them all the kind of lifestyle most families could only dream of. Graham was well aware of the fact that his inheritance had allowed him to open his own architectural firm in Austin at a time when many of his contemporaries were still struggling to pay off school loans.

"And it will be again," Michael said adamantly. "But there's a lot of new competition for the kind of specialized engines we build, and to stay ahead of the game, we've got to become more innovative with our designs. Research and development is expensive. We need an infusion of cash right now, which is why Terrence is proposing selling off some of the family assets rather than incur more debt."

"We own property besides Dad's ranch. The downtown warehouses have got to be worth a small fortune."

"Only if you hold out long enough to find the right buyer. Terrence already has someone interested in the ranch. These guys will fork over a check as soon as the papers are signed. We could have that money in a matter of days."

"I'm not trying to be difficult about this, but—"

"But what?" Michael cut him off impatiently. "The deal makes sense and you know it. Hey, I like playing cowboy as much as the next guy, but we're all adults now with busy lives. When's the last time you drove out there?"

Graham couldn't remember the last time. Still, he was hesitant. "Dad loved that ranch. I don't feel right selling off something that he put his heart and soul into."

"The ranch was a hobby at best. He put his heart and soul into Hollister Motors. He'd be all for this plan and you know it." Michael's gaze hardened. "The company needs that money. If you're holding out just to spite your brother—"

"Give me a little more credit than that," Graham said angrily. "I was blindsided this afternoon. I had no idea Terrence was even considering selling off assets, let alone the ranch. Maybe if I'd been given some warning instead of having papers shoved under my nose and ordered to sign, I might have been a little more agreeable."

"He went about it the wrong way, no question. But what else is new? Terrence is a straightforward kind of guy. Forget how it was put to you. You've had time to mull it over, and you know what's at stake if we don't sell."

"Why didn't Terrence tell me all this himself?"

Michael drained his champagne and reached for another. "Because he's as mule-headed as you are. And he probably didn't want to admit that the company's hit a rough spot. Not to you. Not after all this." He turned toward the windows and gestured with his hand at the twinkling lights of the Houston skyline. "You've got it all, Graham. You've *won*. Now you can afford to be generous. Especially when it comes to family."

Graham shoved his glasses up his nose as he studied the skyline. He didn't feel as if he'd won anything. He'd busted his ass to get where he was today. And, yes, Hollister money had helped him get there faster, but he didn't appreciate Michael's implication that his success was the result of some kind of contest with his brother.

"I just wish someone had told me before now how bad things were at the company," he muttered.

Michael glanced over at him. "Does that mean you'll sign the papers?"

"Of course, I'll sign. The company means a lot to our family."

Michael let out a breath of relief. "We never had this conversation."

Graham shrugged. "Fine. Then I guess you'll want me to tell Terrence the news."

"What news?"

Graham turned in surprise. He hadn't expected his brother to show up tonight even though he and his wife, Ellie, had been issued invitations weeks ago.

Graham felt the same old pang of resentment he always experienced in his brother's presence. Terrence was three years older, and, right up until Graham had turned eighteen, he'd been at least three inches taller. A late growing spurt had put Graham at eye level with his brother, but somehow he still had the impression of having to look up to him.

Growing up, Terrence had been everything that Graham was not. A star athlete with almost palpable charisma, he'd been big man on campus in both high school and college while Graham had been hardly more than his quiet, more intellectual shadow.

Terrence was just like their father and Graham had always envied their closeness. But no matter how hard he tried, there had always been a distance between him and the old man.

Rugged, handsome, and gregarious, Nate Hollister had been a real man's man. He hadn't known how to relate to a son who didn't excel at sports and who spent most of his free time in his room studying and reading.

Graham swallowed past his resentment and smiled. "I'm glad you guys came tonight."

"We wouldn't have missed it for the world." Ellie stood on tiptoes to brush her lips against Graham's cheek. "This place is amazing. I've watched it go up from the day the slab was poured, but seeing it now all lit up against the skyline and knowing that you designed it…" She trailed off with a shiver and held up her arm. "See? I've got goose bumps."

Graham laughed and gave her a light hug. No matter how awkward and uncomfortable he often felt in his brother's presence, Ellie had a way of making him relax. She was seven months pregnant with their third child and it obviously agreed with her. Her eyes and complexion glowed as she beamed up at him. Tiny and blond, she was still as lovely at thirty-eight as she had been back in high school when she and Terrence had been voted the most popular couple.

"I didn't exactly do it on my own," Graham said. "I had a little help."

"It was still your vision. We're all so proud of you. Aren't we, Terry?"

His brother's gaze didn't quite meet Graham's. "I'm just sorry Mom couldn't be here tonight."

"She's where she needs be." Their grandmother had fallen a few days earlier and broken a hip. Their mother, Audrey, had driven up to Lufkin to be with the older woman while she underwent surgery and physical therapy.

Michael placed his hand on Graham's shoulder, a friendly reminder of their earlier conversation. "I need to mingle. I'll see you later."

After he was gone, Graham and Ellie chatted for a few minutes while Terrence watched the crowd with a brooding scowl. When there was a lull in the conversation, Graham said, "I've had time to think about our earlier discussion. I'd like to drop by and sign the papers in the morning before Kendall and I head back to Austin. That is, if you've got time to see me."

Terrence's gaze narrowed. "Are you sure you want to do this? Once those papers are signed, it'll be a done deal. I don't need you coming back in a few days accusing me of having railroaded you into this."

"I'm sure," Graham said, trying to tamp down a spurt of anger at his brother's tone. "I don't know why I was so resistant this afternoon. It just made me think of Dad—"

"Yeah, I know."

Their gazes finally met, and for the first time in a long time, an unspoken understanding passed between them.

Ellie, who was never one to allow a silence to grow awkward, slipped her arm through her husband's. "I'm dying for a drink, honey, and I haven't seen anything all night except champagne." She patted her stomach. "Do you think you could find me a ginger ale?"

"Sure. Be right back."

Once Terrence disappeared, Ellie moved closer to Graham. "Thank you."

"For what?"

"You know for what."

He shrugged. "Like I said, I should never have been so resistant."

"And Terry shouldn't have been so pushy. I know how he gets. Especially with you. He's like a bulldozer."

"It's not just him. We rub each other the wrong way. Always have and probably always will."

"That makes me so sad."

Graham smiled. "Don't let it get to you. It's just the way things are."

"But it *shouldn't* be that way. You two are brothers. You should be closer. Especially now that—"

"Now that what?" Graham asked curiously.

She hesitated, her gaze scanning the crowd. "Now that you have a new niece or nephew on the way," she murmured.

"I can still be a doting uncle, just like I am with Ashley and Caitlin."

Ellie and Terrence's two daughters were ten years apart. Ashley was fifteen going on thirty, a blue-eyed blonde who looked just like her delicate mother but with her father's propensity for hell-raising. That she was causing Terrence the same kind of grief he'd put their mother through at the same age was completely lost on him. It was strange because when they'd been teenagers, Graham had never been able to relate to Terrence's rebellion, but now he was often the one Ashley turned to for advice.

The younger girl, Caitlin, not only looked like her mother, but also had Ellie's sweet disposition. Nothing ever seemed to faze the five-year-old, even the occasional scream fests between her father and older sister.

And now they had another one on the way. Graham loved his nieces dearly, but sometimes after they'd all been together for a holiday or birthday, he was left wondering if he was cut out to be a father. He hadn't said anything to Kendall about his doubts, but he might have to because lately she'd been bringing up the subject of children a lot.

"Where's Kendall?" Ellie asked as if reading his mind.

"I've been wondering the same thing. She went to powder her nose a little while ago and I haven't seen her since."

"Is she okay?"

"Why wouldn't she be?"

Ellie hesitated. "We had lunch today and she seemed—I don't know—quiet. She said she felt fine, but I thought she looked a little stressed."

"She's probably just worn herself out making all the arrangements for our trip."

"Oh, yes, that trip." Ellie sighed. "I'm so envious. What I wouldn't give if Terry and I could get away for a whole month. But once you have kids, everything changes. I doubt we'll be able to manage more than a weekend getaway for the next eighteen years." She adjusted her beaded jacket over her stomach. "Sometimes I wonder what we were thinking. Then again…thinking had very little to do with it." She paused with a chuckle. "You know, a trip like that…just the two of you…I wouldn't be surprised if Kendall came home pregnant."

Graham almost choked on his champagne.

She laughed again. "You'd better get used to the idea of being a daddy, Graham, because I think your lovely wife is ready. More than ready."

Graham felt a sinking sensation in the pit of his stomach. Was that why Kendall had been so emotional recently? "She's not…she didn't tell you…"

"Listen to you stammer! She didn't tell me she was pregnant, no. But I don't know why you're freaking out at the possibility. You'd be a terrific father."

"Not every couple wants to have children," Graham said with a scowl.

"That's true. But I'm pretty sure Kendall does."

"She said that?"

Ellie shrugged. "Not in so many words, but I can tell. It's none of my business, of course…"

"Oh, come on," Graham said dryly. "Since when has that ever stopped you?"

"True. Okay, I'll just say it. Is everything okay between you two? Is there some reason why you don't want to start a family just yet?"

"Everything's fine. We've never been better. And maybe that's what scares me," Graham admitted. "Things are so good between us, I don't want our relationship to change."

"It could be a change for the better, you know. I may complain about being tied down, but I wouldn't take anything for my girls. And Terrence...well, you know how he feels about them."

"I'm not Terrence."

"No, you're not." She gave him an amused look. "I wonder if I should tell you something."

Graham groaned. "Why do I feel as if this conversation has led me straight into a minefield?"

"Relax. It doesn't have anything to do with having babies." Her blue eyes sparkled. "Did you know I used to have a little crush on you in high school?"

"Oh, right. Your boyfriend's geeky younger brother."

"You weren't geeky. You were deep. And don't think I didn't notice how you looked in that football uniform."

"How could you tell? I never got off the bench. Whereas Terrence—"

"Oh, your brother was something all right and I was crazy about him. But you had something special. A quiet kind of confidence that made me think you'd be the person I'd run to if I were ever in trouble. You still have that quality, Graham."

He gave her a rueful look. "You give me far too much credit. Terrence is the hero type, not me."

She reached up and patted his cheek. "That's one of the things I've always adored about you. You're totally oblivious to your appeal. Kendall is one very lucky woman. I hope she knows that."

No, I'm the lucky one, Graham thought, his gaze returning to the crowd. And now if he could just find his wife, the evening would be perfect.

A LITTLE WHILE later, Graham finally spotted Kendall in the crowd. Her red dress stood out like a beacon amidst the sea of black tuxedoes and ball gowns, and his focus vectored in and lingered for the longest moment as he sipped his champagne and tried to hide a sudden impatience.

He would have preferred to do more than admire his wife from afar, but anything other than a smile would have to wait until they got back to the hotel.

He shifted restlessly as he continued to watch her. She was tall and elegant and so graceful she appeared to float through the room. Up close, the scars from the accident were still visible, but rather than detracting from her looks, the imperfections gave her a fragile, ethereal beauty that served to remind Graham of how fleeting life could be. How important it was to live each moment as though it were the last.

Ellie and Terrence had disappeared a few minutes ago, and now Graham stood alone and pensive. He'd lost his enthusiasm for the event and wondered when he and Kendall could slip away. It was all he could do to keep from glancing at his watch, but he told himself that he should just relax. After all, it wasn't every day a man realized a lifelong dream.

As the architect on record for the project, Graham had been invited to say a few words to the crowd, but he'd declined so that the guest of honor—the Mexican ambassador to the United States—would have more time at the podium. Manuel Garza was just winding up his speech. He had close ties to PemCo Oil and had been a strong advocate of deregulating Mexico's petroleum industry to allow in foreign investors. He'd seized the opportunity to stress the necessity of developing a regional energy program and cited the PemCo Tower as a symbolic merger of the two great neighbors. It was a gutsy speech, considering the protests back home.

As the ambassador began to close, Graham's attention drifted to the windows and to the panoramic view of the city. Even now, standing at the very pinnacle of his dream, he could scarcely believe he'd accomplished what he had set out to do—make his mark on the skyline of his hometown.

As he'd told Ellie earlier, the accomplishment was not his alone. Austin-based Hollister and Associates had collaborated on the design with a larger architectural firm in Houston, as well as with the developer, builder and representatives from PemCo Oil.

Thousands of hours had gone into both the design and construction of the building, but all that was behind Graham now. When he walked out of the building tonight, his role in the project would be greatly diminished. He and Kendall would finally be able to enjoy the vacation they'd been talking about for years. A month-long adventure that would take them to Bora Bora, Hong Kong, Singapore and finally the Australian outback.

The tickets and itinerary, along with their passports, were tucked away in his desk drawer at home, their suitcases had been brought down from the attic and Kendall had been feverishly shopping for weeks.

From the parade of sundresses, shoes and sportswear that had been modeled in their bedroom night after night, the one thing that stood out in Graham's memory was a certain turquoise bikini that made him anticipate even more keenly the long, luxurious days on a private island in the South Pacific that would launch the trip.

He could picture Kendall's long, toned body stretched out on the sand, her skin warm and silky to his touch. The image was so vivid that Graham could almost smell the coconut oil, but the stirring of warmth in the lower part of his body was all too real. He needed to think about something else.

You know, a trip like that…just the two of you…I wouldn't be surprised if Kendall came home pregnant.

His thoughts skidded to a halt as his sister-in-law's prediction rushed through his head. How would he feel about that? Graham wondered. He'd never thought of himself as the paternal type, but deep down, he knew that wasn't the real reason for his hesitancy.

After five years of marital bliss, he still harbored a secret doubt about his relationship with Kendall. What if she decided to leave him again?

His gaze went back to her. He couldn't help it. He loved looking at her. But as she drifted closer, he noticed something he hadn't been able to see from a distance. The anxious glitter in her dark eyes might have gone unnoticed if he hadn't been watching her so closely. She was still smiling, but tension tightened the corners of her mouth and her fingers strayed to the gold necklace at her throat, a sure sign that she was upset.

She stopped for a moment, waylaid by someone Graham didn't know, and as the man leaned in to make himself heard over the ambassador, Kendall's gaze uneasily searched the room. Her eyes found Graham, moved away, then came back, a silent plea emanating from the brown depths.

Something was wrong. Graham could see the distress on her face. He started toward her, but at the same moment, a waiter collided with someone in front of him. The heavy tray of crystal flutes toppled, showering champagne over those in the immediate vicinity.

A collective gasp rose from the crowd as everyone scurried out of the way, and Graham's view of Kendall was momentarily blocked.

Somewhere nearby a woman screamed. Not the shocked squeal of someone who had been doused by champagne, but a horrified, ear-splitting shriek that stunned the room into silence.

Everyone seemed to drop back a step, creating a void at the front of the room where a man had collapsed. Graham recognized him instantly. It was Manuel Garza.

Graham's first thought was that the man had had a heart attack as he left the podium, but then he saw a crimson puddle beneath Garza's left shoulder.

The ambassador's wife was on her knees beside him, her hands covered in blood. She looked up, her eyes frantic and brimming. *"Por favor! Someone help him!"*

Graham reacted instinctively. He moved forward, not really knowing what he could do, but in the space of a heartbeat, security came out of the woodwork. Graham was pushed back into the crowd by a man wearing an earpiece. As the officer spoke rapidly into a transmitter concealed by his sleeve, he turned away, and Graham saw someone else rush toward the wounded man.

A hand reached out and grabbed her, but she jerked free and shouted, "For God's sake, I'm a doctor! Let me help him!"

The ambassador's personal bodyguards quickly formed a protective circle around him as the undercover HPD officers assigned to the event moved to restore order. But in the initial pandemonium, Graham had lost sight of Kendall.

He turned now, desperate to find her. He couldn't see her at first, but then he spotted a splash of red near the entrance.

"Kendall!"

Whether she somehow heard him over the roar of the panicked crowd, or whether the force of his gaze drew her attention, Graham didn't know. But at that exact moment, she glanced back, her gaze clinging to his a split second before he found himself pushed back against the wall.

He called out to Kendall, but his voice was lost in the din. Frantic to reach her, Graham tore himself free and fought his way through the terrified mob.

But by the time he reached the door, his wife had vanished.

Chapter Two

Kendall had no idea what had just happened in the room behind her. She'd heard the crash of glass, a scream and then all hell broke loose. She glanced over her shoulder, trying desperately to find Graham again, but someone grabbed her arm and pulled her into the hallway.

"Hurry!" the man ordered in a raspy voice. "This way!"

"Wait!" Kendall tried to resist, but he was too strong.

"I told you. Do as I say and nobody gets hurt." He shoved her toward the elevators, and when she stumbled, he grabbed her arm again and jerked her upright.

Dread tightened in her chest. She hadn't seen or heard from Hector Reyes in years, not since the night she'd tried to flee Mexico for good. Not since the horrible car accident that had left her battered and scarred and wanting to die.

And then she'd opened her eyes one morning and

found Graham at her bedside. She'd later learned from the doctors that she'd been unconscious for nearly a week before his arrival and had been given very little hope of survival. But somehow she must have sensed Graham's presence. Somehow his voice had lured her from the darkness.

For days, he remained at her bedside, talking to her softly when he thought she'd drifted off. He'd been candid about the ambiguity of his feelings, perhaps because he wasn't sure if she could actually comprehend what he was saying.

But she'd heard every word. Lying flat on her back with her face and head swathed in bandages, both arms broken and one leg in traction, drugs dulling but not obliterating the constant pain, she'd listened. And she'd wondered how any woman in her right mind could have ever allowed a man like Graham Hollister to slip away from her.

She'd vowed to herself over and over that if she was lucky enough to survive her wounds, if she was fortunate enough to have a chance to start over, she would do everything in her power to change, to become the kind of person a man like Graham deserved.

But she should have known that the past—those terrible secrets—would eventually catch up with her. That her life before the reconciliation would come back to haunt her. And just when they were thinking of starting a family.

Kendall blinked back hot tears as she stepped into

the elevator. She didn't look at the man beside her. She couldn't.

"I told you where the money is. Take it and let me go," she pleaded.

He was a tall, swarthy man with gleaming black eyes and flawless English. "What assurance do I have that the police won't be waiting for me at the drop point?"

"I wouldn't do that. You know I wouldn't. There's too much at stake. If anyone were ever to find out—"

He laughed. "Yes, you've covered your tracks well, haven't you? You've always been very clever. I'll give you that." His voice hardened. "But the answer is no. You're coming with me. Once I have the money, I'll let you go."

"Can I at least call my husband and tell him I'm okay? He'll know something is wrong. I would never leave without telling him."

"You'll call him as soon as we're safely out of the building. Trust me, you don't want him to follow us. The situation could get very nasty."

Kendall closed her eyes. "Please don't hurt him—"

"As I said, no one will get hurt as long as you cooperate. So just relax and enjoy the ride. It'll soon be over."

"How soon?"

"As soon as I know you haven't betrayed me. Because we both know what you are capable of, do we not?"

She suppressed another shiver as she felt his gaze sweep over her. Hector Reyes had once been employed by the same man she'd worked for in Mexico. Leo Kittering was an American ex-pat who had remarried well and used his wife's resources to forge a powerful empire.

At one time, he'd been a major power broker, but then his only son had died, and all Kittering had been able to focus on was revenge.

Whether Hector Reyes still worked for him or not, she didn't know, but she had a feeling that if Kittering had sent him, she would already be dead. Collecting a hundred thousand dollars in extortion money would not even be on Leo Kittering's radar.

The elevator slid to a stop on the third floor. They got off and used the stairwell to reach the lobby level.

Hector seemed to know his way around very well. He led her quickly down a narrow corridor to an emergency exit that opened into a dead end street.

Kendall braced herself for the alarm she thought would go off when the emergency door was opened, but all remained silent. She wondered if the system had somehow been disengaged, either by Hector or perhaps an accomplice inside the building.

A black van, nearly invisible in the shadowy alley, waited nearby and inched forward as they emerged from the building. A panel slid open in the side, and Hector pushed her toward the vehicle.

As Kendall stumbled forward, someone inside the van grabbed her and pulled her inside. Hector scrambled in behind her, shoved the door closed and the van took off so abruptly, Kendall lost her balance and fell.

Huddled on the floor, she glanced around. Besides Hector and the driver, there were two other men in the back of the van, masked and armed with assault rifles. They spoke in Spanish, so low and rapid that Kendall had trouble following the conversation, even though she'd once lived in Mexico.

But she had no trouble interpreting the danger she suddenly found herself in. This was no ordinary extortion or blackmail scheme. She was being kidnapped. Obviously, the money that Hector had asked for had been a diversion, a way to get and keep her off guard. Now they would go to Graham. He would find out everything.

But it wouldn't matter because she would be dead.

Kendall wasn't naive enough to believe they would release her once they had what they wanted. She knew her chances.

Panic mushroomed in her throat, and it was all she could do to swallow a scream. How was she going to get away from them?

Hector picked up her evening bag, removed her cell phone and tossed it toward her. "Call your husband. Tell him you are all right and you want him to meet you at home."

"But we're spending the night in Houston—"

"Do it!"

Kendall mustered up a cool defiance. "Why should I? If you had any intention of letting me go, you would have taken the money and run."

"Now you are being too clever for your own good," Hector advised. "If you don't do exactly as I say, this will end very badly for you. And for your husband."

At the threat to Graham, Kendall's courage flagged. "What do you want?" she said raggedly. "If it's more money—"

"Some things are more important than money," one of the men barked, his lips curling in disgust. He was tall and dark, with the cruelest eyes Kendall had ever looked into. "But someone like you would have a difficult time comprehending that."

"What do you want from—"

"Enough!" The man hit her with the back of his hand, and Kendall fell back, stunned by the pain. Light exploded behind her eyes, and for a moment, she thought she would pass out.

Hector Reyes knelt beside her and leaning in very close, he placed his lips against her ear. "These men will kill us both if you don't do as I tell you," he whispered, curling her fingers around the cell phone he placed in her limp hand. "They'll put a bullet in my skull, but you won't be so lucky. *Comprende?*"

SECURITY moved quickly to seal the exits, but in the initial confusion, Graham managed to slip out of the room without being detained. He hurried down the long corridor, not knowing if Kendall had come this way or not. Or if he would be stopped before he reached the elevators. All he knew was that he had to find her.

He had no idea who the man was that she'd left with, but Graham's first panicked thought was that the stranger was somehow connected to the attack on the ambassador. And he'd taken Kendall hostage.

But he didn't see how that was possible. The man had been nowhere near Garza when he collapsed.

Something else niggled at Graham. When Kendall turned at the door, their gazes had clung for a moment before he'd been pushed back against the wall. But in that split second, he'd seen her face clearly. She'd looked pale and anxious, but she hadn't been frightened.

A chill slid down Graham's spine as he hurried toward the elevators. The notion that Kendall had left with the stranger of her own accord filled him with the darkest dread even as he told himself there had to be a logical explanation for her behavior.

When she'd walked out before, Graham had been all too willing to take the easy way out, to bury himself in his work and let their relationship drift toward divorce.

But in the five years since the reconciliation, their marriage had grown stronger every day. Or so he'd thought.

Now doubt tore through his heart, and he remembered all the hours that he'd devoted to the PemCo Oil project. All the evenings he couldn't make it home for dinner. The trips. The cancelled plans. Had his wife again grown restless while he pursued his dream?

He would have known if she were that unhappy. They were so close. They talked every day, no matter how busy his schedule. There had to be a perfectly innocent reason for her hasty departure. There had to be—

The vibration of his cell phone inside his breast pocket cut off Graham's thoughts, and as he pulled out the phone, he glanced at the display. It was Kendall.

Relief washed over him as he lifted the phone to his ear. "Kendall?" When she didn't answer, Graham said anxiously, "Are you all right? Where are you?"

Still more silence. Then finally she whispered, "I'm so sorry."

"Sorry for what? Why did you leave like that?"

"I had to." Her voice was low and shaky and Graham knew that something was very wrong.

"Are you sick? Why didn't you tell me? We could have left together."

"I didn't want to tear you away. This is your night, Graham. And I'm sorry I ruined it."

"I don't give a damn about that. Just tell me what's happened? Where are you?"

"I never wanted to hurt you. You have to believe that."

"Tell me what's going on, Kendall. You're scaring the hell out of me."

"I've done things, Graham. Things you don't know anything about. But it was a long time ago. I'm not the same person I was back then. I've changed because of you."

His grip tightened on the phone. "Listen to me. I don't care what you did in the past. We've both made mistakes. Whatever it is, we can work it out."

"Not this time."

"Don't say that."

"I love you—" Her voice broke and Graham heard a male voice mutter something in the background.

"Who's with you?" he demanded.

"No one. It's not what you think."

"I don't know what to think! Just tell me where you are. I'll come get you. We can talk this out. Whatever it is, it can't be that bad."

He heard her draw a shaky breath. "Do you really mean that?"

"Of course I do."

"Then meet me at home. I'll tell you everything. We'll see then if you still want to work it out."

The connection went dead and Graham immediately tried to call her back. Her phone rang and rang, but she'd obviously turned it off.

Cursing inwardly, Graham started toward the elevator, then stopped as the walls started to spin. He recognized the symptoms—it was an old problem—

but this time the vertigo had come on so suddenly, he'd had no time to prepare, no time to focus. He could feel the eighty-five-story building sway as the walls tilted and the floor seemed to disappear beneath him.

For a moment, he imagined himself standing on one of the steel support beams, and he blindly put out a hand to steady himself. That was when he saw Kendall's earring lying on the floor in front of the elevators. He knew it was hers because he'd given her the pear-shaped rubies as an early anniversary present.

The earring must have fallen off as she got onto the elevator. Or had she left it on purpose as some sort of clue to alert Graham that she hadn't left of her own free will?

He was grasping at straws, Graham realized. Kendall hadn't been coerced into leaving. He'd seen her at the door. The look in her eyes when she'd glanced back hadn't been fear. It had been regret and Graham had no idea why.

Graham's head was still spinning, but he knew he had to somehow get the vertigo under control. He would force himself to function because he had to. He had to find Kendall.

Clutching the earring in one hand, he stumbled toward the elevator, punched the down button and waited for the doors to slide open. As he staggered into the confined space, he stood with his back pressed against the wall, his gaze focused on the red emergency button. He didn't look at anything else, and eventually the walls stopped spinning. His head cleared and by the time he reached the lobby, he'd managed to regain control of his equilibrium.

The huge glass-and-granite lobby was already swarming with police officers. Through the wall of windows he could see the bubblegum lights whirling atop the squad cars, and as he watched, a SWAT van pulled to the curb. Several men in armored body suits piled out of the back and headed toward the building with grim, determined expressions.

Graham quickly canvassed the lobby. Luckily no one had noticed him yet, but he hadn't taken the time to figure out what his next move should be, let alone formulate any kind of plan. Obviously, he wasn't getting out of the building without being seen, and even if he could, he had no way of knowing whether Kendall was still inside. But his gut told him that she was already gone, and he had a terrible feeling that if he didn't find her soon, she would be lost to him forever.

Graham continued to study the lobby until he saw a familiar face. Earlier, when he and Kendall had first arrived, he'd struck up a brief conversation with one of the security guards. He'd manned the desk where all guests were required to sign in, and behind him, a bank of screens monitored the exits and various points inside the building.

Graham had caught a glimpse of an Astros game on one of the screens, and he'd asked the guard for the score. The man had recognized Graham's name when he signed in, and they'd talked for several minutes about baseball and the design of the building before Graham realized that Kendall had gone over to the elevators to wait.

That same guard was still behind the desk as he watched the controlled chaos in the lobby.

Straightening his tie and then his glasses, Graham strode toward the guard without looking right or left. His formal attire would hardly allow him to blend in with the dour-faced officers in the lobby, but more often than not an air of authority was all it took. He'd learned that lesson first from his father and then from his brother.

The guard didn't seem to notice as Graham approached. His attention was riveted on the SWAT activity outside the front doors.

Graham cleared his throat and stood a little straighter. "Excuse me."

The guard turned. "Something I can help you with?" He was short and stocky, with thick blond hair and a round, boyish face.

"I hope so," Graham said. "Do you remember me? We spoke earlier when I first came in. I asked you about the baseball game."

"Oh, yeah. You're the architect, right?

"That's right. Graham Hollister."

"What are you doing down here? I thought they were holding everyone upstairs." The guard nodded toward the elevators as he hitched up his pants. He had the kind of protruding midsection that made it difficult to keep the waist of his pants from sliding down. He also wore glasses with thick black rims. He reminded Graham of a comedian who used to be on TV.

"I left before they locked the doors."

The guard's attention perked up. "Were you up there when it happened?"

"Yes, but I didn't really see anything. There were too many people around."

"Doesn't matter. The cops are going to want to talk to you anyway. They'll want to talk to everybody who was in that room."

"I understand that, but I'm looking for my wife," Graham explained. "I just want to make sure she's all right. She came down a few minutes ahead of me. I need to know if she left the building before I arrived."

"Not likely. HPD has the place surrounded. Nobody's allowed in or out."

"She may have gotten out before the lockdown. You saw her earlier when we came in. She's wearing a red dress. Tall, slim, brunette. Very attractive. She may have had a man with her."

The guard gave Graham a curious look. "She didn't come through the lobby. I'm sure I would have noticed."

"What about the other exits?"

"The front entrance was the only one open tonight. The others were locked for the evening. And even if they weren't, I monitor all the exits from the console. I would have seen her, regardless."

"Maybe you stepped away from your desk for a moment. Went to the bathroom or something."

"Been right here all night."

The guard was starting to get a little impatient, and if Graham wasn't careful, he might not get anything else out of him. "Look, could you just please check the surveillance recording? It won't take long."

"I'm not authorized to do that." The guard's voice noticeably chilled. "Besides, I've already told you. Your wife didn't come through the lobby. She didn't leave the building through the front exit or any exit. I would have seen her. If she left the party upstairs with some guy, maybe they're just having a cozy little chat somewhere in the building."

He started to turn away, but Graham grabbed his arm. "Wait!"

The guard jerked away from Graham's grasp. "Hey, take it easy, buddy. The feds are in control now, okay? I couldn't help you out even if I wanted to. Now back off before I call a cop over here and have him personally escort you upstairs."

The guard's agitation attracted the attention of two men standing nearby. One was tall, thin and impeccably dressed in a dark suit while the other was shorter, stockier and more rumpled. But they both wore buzz cuts and the unmistakable air of federal authority.

The taller one said something to his partner and then strode over to where Graham stood with the security guard. "Something wrong here?"

His tone was low and amicable, but his eyes glinted with steel. He had the look of a regimented man, from his precisely knotted tie to his spit-shined loafers, and Graham knew instinctively that the guy was not someone he'd want for an enemy.

"I'm Special Agent Delacourt with the Federal Bureau of Investigation." He flashed his ID and badge. "What seems to be the problem?"

The guard spoke before Graham had a chance to. "This man says his wife is missing. He wants to look at the security tapes so that he can see if she left the building."

The hard eyes turned back to Graham. "When did she leave?"

"She wasn't feeling well earlier. She came down for some fresh air. I just want to make sure she's all right," Graham said.

"You have some identification?"

"Of course."

While Graham fished his wallet out of his jacket, the security guard said helpfully, "He's the architect who designed this building."

Delacourt cocked his head. "That right?

"Yes. My name is Graham Hollister." He handed his driver's license to the agent.

Delacourt glanced at it briefly, then called his partner over. "Becker, you still got that guest list HPD's circulating?"

The shorter agent strode toward them. "What's going on?"

"See if you can find Graham Hollister on it."

While his partner scrutinized a sheet of paper, Delacourt refocused his attention on Graham. "You were at the reception when the shooting occurred?"

"Yes."

"Did you see it happen?"

"No. There were too many people around. The only thing I saw was the ambassador lying on the floor in a pool of blood. Do you know anything about his condition? Is he going to be okay?"

"We don't know yet. Did you notice anything unusual before the shooting occurred?"

Graham didn't like the way Delacourt was looking at him. It was almost as if he suspected Graham of something. "A waiter dropped a tray of glasses right before it happened. It caused a commotion."

Delacourt and Becker exchanged glances. "Anything else you can think of?"

"Not right offhand. Like I said, it was crowded and I wasn't really paying attention."

"Graham Hollister's on the list all right," Becker confirmed.

"He says he's the architect that designed the building," Delacourt said.

Becker's brows rose. "Oh, yeah? That's convenient."

"Isn't it?" Delacourt turned back to Graham. "We're going to need you to come with us."

Graham frowned. "Why? I haven't done anything wrong."

Delacourt and Becker exchanged another glance. "No one is suggesting that you did."

"Then why do you need me?"

"We're going to search this building from the ground up. You can save us a lot of time by going over the blueprints with some of our agents."

"But—"

Delacourt gave him the hard look again. "Maybe you didn't understand me. No one is leaving here until we've searched the entire building. The sooner we get started, the sooner you can get out of here and go find your wife."

The last thing Graham wanted was to be tied up for hours, but he didn't have a choice. He nodded wearily and followed the agents across the lobby.

Chapter Three

Graham had been sequestered for nearly three hours with a team of FBI agents, State Department officials and HPD officers when Delacourt came in suddenly and announced that he was free to go.

"Does this mean you've found the shooter?" Graham asked as the special agent escorted him to the front entrance.

"Let's just say, we no longer think the suspect is in the building."

"Why?"

"We have our reasons."

Graham wondered what those reasons were, but he decided that for now it was best to say as little as possible. Until he could find out what was going on with Kendall, the last thing he needed was Delacourt's continued interest.

"What about the ambassador? How's he doing?"

"Holding his own. That's about all I can say." Delacourt nodded to another agent in the lobby.

"You haven't remembered anything else that might help us out?"

Graham shrugged. "Like I said, there was a lot of confusion. I didn't even know Garza had been wounded. I didn't hear a gunshot, although I suppose it could have been masked by the falling tray. I thought at first he'd collapsed from a heart attack. And then I saw the blood on the floor beneath him. That's all I remember."

"What about the waiter who dropped the tray? You said he had dark hair, an average build. Any distinguishing marks? Scars, moles anything at all that you can recall?"

Graham shook his head. "Nothing more than what I've already told you. I didn't really get a good look at him. After he dropped the tray, everyone around him scrambled to get out of the way. And then a second or two later, I saw the ambassador lying on the floor."

The agent fished in his pocket and brought out a card. "Details sometime come back once the adrenaline settles. If you think of anything, no matter how insignificant it may seem, give me a call at this number."

Graham pocketed the card and nodded. "I will."

He started to walk away, but Delacourt said suddenly, "Hey, what about your wife? Have you heard from her?"

"No, not since earlier. I guess I'm meeting her at home."

As Graham walked away, he resisted the urge to glance over his shoulder. He had a strange feeling that Delacourt was standing there watching him. And that he would be hearing from the agent again very soon.

As GRAHAM climbed behind the wheel of his BMW a little while later, he started thinking again about Kendall's strange exit from the reception. And he thought about the way she'd left all those years ago, with only a note to explain her sudden departure. She'd disappeared for months with barely any communication. Graham had had to learn from his best friend that she'd moved to Mexico.

Back then, Kendall had been a woman he barely knew. A gorgeous, restless creature who had grown tired of her husband's fifteen-hour workdays. And it wasn't as though Graham hadn't seen it coming. He had. He just hadn't done anything about it. And now this.

What if she decided to leave him again?

He cut himself off. He wouldn't go there. Not until he talked to her.

The other guests had long since left the building, and the parking garage was nearly deserted. As Graham backed out of his slot, he took out his cell phone and started placing calls.

He checked the hotel first. He and Kendall had booked a suite at the Warwick for the night so they wouldn't have to drive all the way back to Austin after the reception. She'd asked to meet at home, but it made more sense that she meant their hotel room.

But she didn't pick up in their suite nor had she left a message. Graham tried his brother's house next and when Ellie answered, he quickly explained why he was calling.

"She left without saying anything? That's odd," Ellie murmured.

"You didn't see her?" Graham asked anxiously.

"I looked for both of you before we left, but after the shooting everything was so chaotic. I was scared to death that some madman was going to open fire into the crowd. It didn't even occur to me at first that it was an assassination attempt..." She trailed off, and Graham could hear the tremble in her voice. "I can see why you're worried about Kendall. I'm still so shaky I don't want to let Terrence or the girls out of my sight. But you say...she left before the shooting? Why would she leave without telling you?"

"I don't know. I was hoping you could tell me. You said she seemed quiet at lunch today. Did she say or do anything that might give me a clue?"

Ellie sighed. "I'm afraid I can't help you, Graham. But I'm sure it's nothing to worry about. She'll turn up. She may even be back at the hotel waiting for you now."

"I just tried the suite. She's not there."

"Well, then, she may be on her way. You've called her cell?"

"Of course, I have. It's turned off."

"Do you want one of us to drive over to the Warwick and check the suite?"

Their house in the Museum District was only a few blocks from the hotel, but Graham was already pulling onto the street. He was waylaid for a moment by a police officer at the garage exit who checked his ID, then waved him on.

"I appreciate the offer, but I'm on my way over there now. I'll check it out for myself."

"Let me know if you hear anything."

"I will. Thanks, Ellie. I'm sure you're right. It's probably nothing. We just got our wires crossed."

But if it was a misunderstanding, he would have heard from her by now. Besides, a simple mix-up wouldn't explain her sudden departure from the reception or the phone call a few minutes later. *I've done things, Graham...*

He drew a breath and wondered why he hadn't told Ellie about that phone call. Maybe because he didn't want to attach too much importance to it, but how could he not? The ominous conversation had been playing in his head for hours, niggling at his peace of mind.

Kendall was gone. And for all Graham knew, she might not be coming back.

He slammed his palm against the steering wheel in frustration. The downtown traffic was still heavy even at that time of night, and he suddenly felt as if every minute that went by put him further away from

Kendall. His first impulse was to drive straight home to Austin where she'd promised to meet him, but he wanted to check their room first.

When he pulled up in front of the Warwick, he didn't bother parking, but instead jumped out and tossed his keys to the valet, telling the young man that he would only be a minute.

He called the room again on his cell phone as he hurried toward the elevator. Still no answer.

As he let himself into their darkened suite, Graham could no longer deny that something was very wrong. He'd been trying for hours to convince himself there had to be a logical explanation for everything that had happened.

But now, standing in the room with the scent of his wife's perfume lingering in the air, he finally admitted to himself that she wasn't just gone. She was very likely in trouble. And he didn't know what in the hell to do about it.

Even though he knew she wasn't there, he went through the suite, calling her name, checking the bedroom, the bathroom and finally the closet. The clothes she'd brought for their overnight trip were still hanging from the rod, her shoes lined up neatly on the floor and her suitcase tucked away in a corner.

She hadn't been back to the room. All her things were exactly the way she'd left them, including the silk robe she'd tossed on the bed earlier as she dressed.

Graham lifted the silk to his face. Her presence in

the room was so palpable he expected her to come walking in at any second.

But she didn't.

He went over to the window and stared out at the city lights as he wondered where on earth she'd gone to. And what he would do if he couldn't find her.

He racked his brain for something—a seemingly throwaway moment perhaps—that would help him. He replayed the entire evening in his head. There had to be something she'd said or done that had alluded to her state of mind.

Earlier, they'd made love before they left for the reception. Had she held him more tightly than usual? Whispered to him a little more desperately? Had she known when they walked out the door that she wouldn't be coming back?

He went over everything time and again, but he kept returning to one moment in particular. Kendall had just come out of the bathroom, the robe belted tightly about her slim waist as she walked over to the closet. But instead of removing her dress, she'd stood for a moment, lost in thought, and a strange look had come over her features. An odd mixture of panic, sadness and resolution.

She hadn't been aware of Graham's scrutiny. He'd stood at the dresser mirror adjusting his tie, but his gaze was on her reflection. Ever since the accident, she'd been uncomfortable in social situations, even though most of the scars had faded. She was a beautiful woman, but Graham knew she still sometimes had doubts about her appearance. The change was just so drastic. Even after all this time, he still sometimes caught her staring at her reflection in the mirror. Now he realized that he had misconstrued her earlier hesitation. He'd thought that she hadn't wanted to attend the reception.

"We don't have to go tonight," he'd told her. "We could just skip this shindig altogether and stay in."

She glanced at him in surprise, whatever emotion she'd felt a moment earlier replaced by a chiding scowl. "You're not going to get out of it that easily. This is your big night and you'll enjoy every minute of it even if it kills you."

Slipping out of the robe, she tossed it onto the bed, then clad only in a strapless bra and matching panties, she took out a red dress and held it up to her slender form as she stood at the full-length mirror.

"New dress?"

"I just got it today."

"Nice color."

"It's a little too flashy for me," she said, her gaze meeting Graham's again, then darting away. "I let Ellie talk me into it," she murmured. "Maybe I shouldn't wear it."

"Maybe you shouldn't wear anything." Graham came up behind her and wrapped his arms around her. "You know I'd much prefer to stay here and celebrate privately."

"I thought we'd just settled that." She playfully tried to push him away, but as his lips moved from her ear to her neck, she shivered. She hung the red dress back in the closet, then turned, winding her arms around his neck. "We really should finish dressing."

"We will in a minute." His fingers undid her bra and the lace dropped to the floor.

"That's your idea of dressing?"

But it was only a half-hearted protest, and she said nothing else as he picked her up and carried her to the bed. Quickly shedding his tuxedo, he lay down beside her, drawing her on top of him as she gave a soft laugh. "We're going to be so late."

"Ask me if I give a damn."

"You should. You've worked so hard for this night. I'm so proud of you. You have no idea—" She broke off, her eyes filling with sudden tears.

"Hey, what's this about?" He reached up and brushed away the moisture from her cheek.

"I'm just so happy being with you. I know it sounds corny, but I never knew I could love someone as much as I love you."

"I love you, too." He rolled her over and propped himself on one elbow as he gazed down at her, his hand lazily stroking a shoulder, a breast and eventually an inner thigh.

She trembled as she curled a hand around the back of his neck and drew him toward her. "You do things to me, Graham." Her voice was a husky whisper in the muted twilight of the bedroom. "Things I never even dreamed possible."

I've done some things, Graham. Things you don't know anything about.

GRAHAM STAYED in the fast lane as he headed west on 290. Once he was free of Houston traffic, he set the cruise control at eighty-five and started placing calls to anyone he could think of who might know of Kendall's whereabouts.

Other than Ellie, she didn't have a lot of close friends. When they were first married, she'd sold real estate for a living and had a very busy social life. But she'd lost touch with many of her friends and clients when she left that job to work in an art gallery in Houston where they'd been living at the time.

The cachet had soon worn off that position, too, and she'd drifted from one job to another until finally she'd given up any pretense of a career. She'd seemed content to occupy herself around the house, which was fine if that had made her happy. She didn't need to work if she didn't want to.

But evidently her discontent had been growing for a long time without Graham ever noticing. After the separation, he'd had no idea of her move to Mexico until Michael called and told him about it. And even then Graham hadn't been all that interested because he'd already relocated to L.A. where he'd been offered an incredible opportunity with one of the country's most prestigious architectural firms.

Now, as the powerful car ate up the miles between Houston and Austin, Graham berated himself for his past indifference and self-absorption. While he'd immersed himself in ambition, he hadn't noticed or cared that his wife had been floundering.

After the accident, they'd settled in Austin where Graham had opened his own firm. Kendall had thrown herself into decorating the house that he'd built on a hillside overlooking the city.

Once that job was finished, he'd been afraid she would fall back into her old, restless ways, but instead she'd gone back to school and gotten a job with a local design firm. She'd surprised Graham—and perhaps even herself—with her dedication.

She seemed to love everything about their life together, so what the hell was going on?

I've done some things, Graham. Things you don't know anything about…

Her confession vibrated through him with every beat of his heart. His knuckles whitened where he clutched the steering wheel, and he was suddenly gripped with an urgency he couldn't explain. All he knew was that he had to get home. If there were any answers, he would find them in the house the two of them had shared so intimately.

SHIELDED BY five acres of wooded grounds and a wrought-iron security fence, the sprawling one-story ranch sat on the eastern slope of a hilly landscape.

The house was both rustic and luxurious, and in the wrong hands, could easily have become ostentatious. But Kendall's restraint had turned it into a comfortable retreat. Everything from the furniture to the drapes to the muted rugs on the hardwood floors had been chosen with an eye toward warmth and grace. As a result, Graham had always loved coming home. Not just to the house, but to the woman whose touch was everywhere.

He wondered if she would be there waiting for him, and he couldn't suppress a leap of hope as the wrought-iron gates swung open. He drove through, anxious to see the beckoning lights of home.

Pulling around the circular drive, he parked in front and jumped out. He let himself inside and saw immediately that the alarm was still engaged and his heart sank.

He called out to Kendall anyway as he tossed his keys into a hand-painted bowl she'd brought back from a trip to Italy the year before. "Are you home?"

Walking through the airy foyer into the living room, he quickly scanned his surroundings, searching for some clue that she'd been there. He could see the courtyard through the French doors, and just beyond the stucco wall, the sparkle of the pool.

"Kendall?"

He went through the entire house, checking the kitchen, the study, the media room and finally the master suite. The bed was neatly made up, the carpet freshly vacuumed. Obviously, their housekeeper, Jacinda, had been there after they'd left the day before, but there was no sign in any of the rooms that Kendall had been home.

Graham stepped back into the hallway. He started toward the living room, then changed his mind and went into his study where he quickly checked his desk drawer for their plane tickets and itinerary.

Everything was just as he'd left it and he let out a breath of relief.

What did you think? That she would take the tickets and leave without you?

Graham didn't know what to think. The whole night was one big mystery, and he was getting more frustrated and worried by the minute.

He hurried out to the garage to check for her car. The silver Jag was still parked exactly where she'd left it and the metal was cool to his touch.

Going back inside, he slowly walked down the hallway to their bedroom again. He had one more thing he needed to check out. He'd almost forgotten all about it.

For Kendall's birthday one year, he'd given her an antique music box. She kept it on the nightstand at her side of the bed. Graham had knocked it off one day and broken the wind-up stem. When he picked it up to examine the damage, he found a safety deposit box key taped to the bottom.

Kendall had been out of town visiting a friend, and Graham had the music box repaired before she got home. He never told her about breaking it or about finding the key. But for the longest time, he couldn't stop thinking about it. Sometimes he'd wake up in the middle of the night, the urge to check and see if the key was still there almost overpowering.

He hadn't needed a shrink to tell him what his problem was. The key symbolized his doubts. It was a physical link to Kendall's secrets, to her past, and even after the reconciliation and the renewal of their vows, Graham still sometimes wondered if what they had was only an illusion.

He drew a breath. The music box was still on the nightstand, exactly where she always kept it. He stared at it from the doorway, seized for a moment by a terrible feeling of what he was about to find out about his wife.

Then he quickly crossed the room and picked up the box. The inlaid cherrywood was smooth and cool to his touch. A few notes of a minuet tinkled in the silence as he turned it over.

The key was still taped to the bottom.

Graham had no idea what might be in Kendall's secret deposit box, and for months after he found the key, he'd been tormented by the possibilities. Now, for some strange reason, the sight of the key reassured him.

Setting the box back on the nightstand, he turned and caught a glimpse of his haggard reflection in the dresser mirror. His hair was mussed, his eyes bloodshot and watery. He looked like death warmed over, as his grandmother liked to say.

He jerked off his tie and unfastened the top button of his shirt, but he didn't feel like taking the time to change. Instead, he retraced his steps down the hallway to the living room and stepped through the French doors into the courtyard. The night was very dark and silent, and he paused for a moment as a strange feeling of being watched came over him.

Graham spun, his gaze scouring the room behind him. The lights were on and he could see most of the living room through the French doors. No one was there. He was letting his imagination get the better of him.

Still, as he walked through the courtyard, circled the pool, then took the path down through the woods to the creek, he couldn't shake the notion that he wasn't alone.

He'd had a summerhouse built near the water, and Kendall sometimes went down there to sit and listen to the stream trickle over the smooth stones. Maybe that was where she was now. Maybe it was her presence that he suddenly felt so strongly.

But she wasn't in the summerhouse. She wasn't anywhere.

Battling both fatigue and panic, Graham strode

back up the stone pathway. He could hear the coyotes in the distance and a chill shot up his spine. Not out of any worry for his safety, but because the eerie sound seemed to echo his growing fear.

He paused in the courtyard with another shiver. Someone was there. He could feel it.

Turning slowly, he saw something move in the shadows. "Kendall?"

The hair on the back of his neck prickled with warning. He stared at the spot for several seconds before he managed to convince himself that he'd seen nothing more than leaves fluttering in a stray breeze.

His cell phone started ringing, and with one last glance over his shoulder, he went back inside. He checked the display before lifting the phone to his ear. It was his brother's number.

"Graham?" Ellie's voice sounded anxious and worried. "Have you heard from Kendall?"

"No, not yet."

"Are you at the hotel?"

"No, I drove back to Austin. I'm home."

"You drove back to Austin? Why?"

"Because I got a call from Kendall earlier and she asked me to meet her here."

"When did she call? After we talked?"

He hesitated, still not certain why he didn't want to come clean with Ellie. She and Kendall were friends and she had a right to know everything. Graham didn't understand his reluctance, but some instinct held him back from disclosing his worst fears. Ellie was pregnant. She didn't need to be dragged into this.

Whatever *this* turned out to be.

"I heard from her a little while ago," he evaded.

"Well, that's good, right?"

"I don't know. Like I said, she asked me to meet her at home, but she's not here."

"I don't understand why she'd want to meet you there," Ellie said. "It doesn't make any sense. You were planning on spending the night in Houston. And besides, you drove here together. How would she get back to Austin without you?"

"I don't know. She didn't give me time to ask that question." Graham raked his fingers through his hair in frustration.

"What do you mean?"

"We were cut off."

"Cut off? You mean she hung up on you?"

"I don't think so."

"Graham…" Ellie's voice trailed off as if she really didn't want to mention what she was suddenly thinking. "I don't know how to put this…"

"Just say it."

"Did you two have a fight? Is that what this is all about?"

"We didn't have a fight. Everything was fine earlier when we left the hotel. Something must have happened at the reception."

Ellie hesitated again, this time with an audible sigh.

"Graham…there's something you need to know. What you just said about everything being fine…that's not really true. When I told you earlier that she was quiet at lunch, I didn't tell you everything."

Graham's heart gave a painful twist. "What are you talking about?"

"I promised her I wouldn't say anything, but under the circumstances—"

"For God's sake, Ellie, tell me!"

"She called me one day last week and asked for money. A loan."

"She *what?*" Graham felt as if he'd been punched in the chest. Suddenly, he had a difficult time breathing.

"I know. It took me by surprise, too."

"Why would she do that?" He gazed out the window. His wife had gone to someone else for a loan. *Why?* They had plenty of money, more than enough to live on for the rest of their lives, and Kendall had full access to their accounts. Why would she ask Ellie for a loan?

The only reason Graham could think of was that she'd needed money for some reason that she didn't want him to know about.

He thought about the key taped to the bottom of the music box. What else was his wife keeping from him?

"How much did she ask for?"

"A hundred thousand dollars."

Graham's mouth dropped. "My God."

Ellie let out a long breath. "I hated not telling you, but I promised her I wouldn't say anything. I asked her why she needed that kind of money, but she wouldn't confide in me. She said the less I knew the better."

Graham didn't even know what to say to that.

"Are you sure the two of you didn't have a fight? Maybe she just wanted to get away for a while," Ellie said hopefully.

"You don't need a hundred thousand dollars to *get away*," Graham said angrily. Not if you plan on coming back. "What did you tell her?"

"The truth. I couldn't get my hands on that kind of money even if I wanted to."

"And what did she say?"

"Nothing. She understood. She said she'd try the bank."

Graham scrubbed a hand down his face. "Why on earth would she need that much money?"

"I have no idea. But yesterday at lunch she was more than subdued, Graham. She was upset. I tried to get her to talk to me, but she said it was something she had to work out on her own. I'm afraid she's in some kind of trouble."

"What kind of trouble?"

"I don't know. But talking to her yesterday was like…."

"What?"

Ellie's voice quivered. "…it was like the old Kendall had come back."

He squeezed his eyes closed. This couldn't be happening. How could he not have known that his own wife was in trouble? Why had he not sensed that something was wrong, that somehow things had changed between them?

"Graham?"

"I'm still here."

"What are you going to do?"

The only thing he could do. "Find her."

"Will you let me know when you do?"

He heard the question, but he didn't respond because his attention was suddenly caught by another movement outside.

Someone was moving stealthily across the courtyard toward the French doors. Graham's first thought was that Kendall had come home.

"I have to go, Ellie. I'll call you later."

He hung up the phone and started toward the doors, not remembering if he'd locked them when he came back in. Then he saw another shadow behind the first. And another. As they got closer to the house, Graham saw them in the light that spilled out from the living room. There were four of them. They wore dark clothing, ski masks and carried assault rifles.

Graham was so stunned that he couldn't move for a moment. Then his adrenaline kicked in and he spun, lunging for the foyer and the front door. He heard a loud crash and the sound of glass shattering behind him as someone kicked in the French doors.

He glanced over his shoulder, and as he saw the armed men streaming into the room, he dove for cover.

Chapter Four

A blast from one of the rifles ripped through the wall behind Graham. The plaster exploded as every window in the house seemed to rattle.

"Stay where you are, Mr. Hollister, or the next time my men won't miss."

The voice was calm, almost pleasant. A strange counterpoint to the violence still echoing through the house.

Slowly, Graham turned toward the stranger. His ears were ringing from the blast, his heart beating so hard his chest felt ready to explode. He was terrified, but he didn't want them to see his fear. They had invaded his home for a reason. If he stayed calm and gave them what they wanted, maybe they'd leave.

But almost instantly he knew it wasn't going to be that easy.

The man who had spoken stepped boldly forward. He was the only one who didn't wear a mask, and he appeared unconcerned about revealing his face.

Which could only mean one thing—Graham wasn't getting out of this alive.

"What do you want?" he tried to ask coolly, but a tremble in his voice gave away his fear.

The man smiled. "Don't be ashamed. You have good reason to be afraid. But rest assured my men and I haven't come here to harm you. We don't want to hurt anyone. As long as you remain calm and do exactly as we ask, everyone will get out of this alive."

"What do you mean, *everyone?*" Graham asked in dread.

The man gestured toward the living room. "We should sit. The explanations could take awhile."

"Who the hell are you? What do you want from me?"

The man sighed. "I can understand how helpless you must be feeling, and I'm not without sympathy. But please believe me when I tell you that your cooperation is imperative. How this night ends is in your hands." The man gestured again toward the living room. "Please, let's sit."

Graham tried to curb his instincts. He wasn't a violent man, but he wasn't a coward, either. He wanted to retaliate for the violation of his home, his sanctuary, but he knew that he wasn't dealing with a simple-minded thug here. He recognized the dead eyes and cruel half smile for what they were—attributes of a soulless man.

He walked over and sat down at one end of the

couch. He was still in shock, but he'd gathered enough of his wits about him to know his only hope was to buy himself some time.

The stranger came over and sat down in a chair opposite the couch. Only a coffee table separated them, and Graham took a moment to memorize the man's features.

He was tall, lean, somewhere in his forties. Like the other men, he was dressed in black, but his attire was much more formal—a dark tailored suit that fitted him like a glove. His face was pitted and scarred, a visage that was both striking and repulsive.

Graham glanced away. He could feel a slight breeze blowing in through the shattered doors and he wanted more than anything to be outside, to be *anywhere* except the nightmare in which he suddenly found himself trapped.

He thought of Kendall and his gaze shot back to the stranger. "You know where my wife is, don't you? That's what this is about. You've come with a ransom demand."

The man continued to smile.

Graham was suddenly filled with rage. He jumped up and lunged toward the stranger. "If you've hurt her—"

Two men were on him in an instant. One of them held his arms behind him while the other hit him with his fist, twice in the face and once very hard in the stomach. Graham's knees folded. As he dropped to the floor, a knee connected with his gut and he doubled over in agony. His glasses fell off and drops of blood splashed against the dark wood floor as he rolled to his side and drew his knees up to his chest.

The pain seemed to go on forever. For the longest time, he struggled even to catch his breath. As he coughed up blood and vomit, he could hear someone laughing. The sound filled him with rage. He wiped his mouth with his sleeve as he staggered to his feet. The pain weakened his legs and he swayed as black spots swam before his eyes. But he would stand even if it killed him because he wouldn't give these animals the satisfaction of seeing him writhe in agony on the floor.

He lifted his head and glared at the stranger for a long moment before he leaned down and picked up his glasses.

"I'm sorry that had to happen," the man said with what sounded like genuine regret. "But it was necessary. You're composed now. You'll sit quietly and listen to everything I have to say."

"Where's my wife?"

"She's safe. For now."

"Where is she?"

"On her way out of the country. You'll never be able to find her. Your only hope of seeing her again is to cooperate with me."

"What do you want?" Blood streamed down Graham's face. He wiped it away with the back of his hand, barely aware of his action. Fury and disgust had replaced his pain.

The stranger leaned forward, offering him a linen handkerchief, but Graham ignored it.

The man sat back against the chair and calmly tucked the hankie back into his pocket. "My name is Gabriel Esteban. You won't have heard of me, but I guarantee after this night, you'll never forget me."

Graham said nothing to that. He made a quick survey of the room, checking the positions of the other three men. They had all the exits covered. He was trapped. He had no recourse but to hear the man out.

"A wise decision," Esteban said, correctly interpreting Graham's darting gaze. "You can't run away from this. You're in it now and there's no turning back."

"In *what?*" Graham demanded, his outrage the only thing keeping him sane at the moment. If he let down his guard…if he stopped for even a moment to contemplate the reality of the situation…

These men had his wife.

His head started to swim, but he willed away the dizziness. He had to focus. Stay in control. Figure a way out so he could find Kendall and end this.

He drew a breath, his gaze on Esteban. "Why don't you stop with the cryptic remarks and just tell me what the hell you want? Money?"

"Yes, of course, I want money. But there are other things I'll want from you as well. Things that won't rest easy with a man like you. That's why we're taking this nice and slow. You'll need time to adjust to your new life. Yes, notice that I said your new life because make no mistake…" Esteban gracefully draped one leg over the other, his dead eyes suddenly taking on a cruel, taunting glint. "The life you knew before tonight is over. You'll never get it back."

Graham's heart started to pound again. The room tilted as the vertigo tugged behind his eyes, undermining his equilibrium. His ears started to ring, but he tried to ignore it. He couldn't have an attack now. He had to concentrate. He had to *think*. Kendall's life depended on how well he handled the situation.

He took off his glasses and tried to wipe away the smudges. "How much do you want?"

"We'll get to the amount later. First, I want to go over the rules with you."

"Rules?"

"Yes, of course. Every game must have rules."

Graham stared at him coldly. "This is a game to you?"

Esteban shrugged. "I enjoy what I do, yes. And I always win. You should accept that and save us both a lot of trouble."

A muscle jerked in Graham's cheek. "What are the rules?"

Esteban nodded his approval at Graham's acceptance. "First, you are to tell no one." As he spoke, he took out a thin, black cigarette and lit up. The smoke was thick and foul in the pristine atmosphere of the house. "Not the police. Not the FBI. Not your family or friends or business associates. *No one.*"

A cloud of smoke floated between them. It burned Graham's eyes, but he resisted the urge to wave it away. Somehow he knew that Esteban would perceive the gesture as another weakness.

"Two. You will not try to find your wife on your own. The effort would be pointless and you would waste a good deal of valuable time and resources. Not to mention my goodwill. As I said earlier, she's on her way out of the country. There's nothing you can do to find her. Nothing other than to cooperate. That is your only hope."

He seemed to be waiting for a response so Graham said, "Go on."

"Three. You will be given a cell phone that must be kept with you at all times. If I can't reach you, no matter the hour, I'm afraid the consequences will be dire."

"Is that it?"

"Hardly." The smile turned sardonic. "We're just getting started."

Esteban stubbed out the cigarette in a crystal bowl on the end table. He took his time, grinding the ashes into the glass as if he were making some kind of point. And very possibly, he was.

"Four. There will be several drops, each to be

arranged at a future time. As I've already mentioned, there will be other requirements that must be met, but for now, you don't need to worry about any of that."

Graham stared at him in disbelief. It was like being trapped in a nightmare from which he couldn't awaken. He didn't know how he was supposed to respond. What he was supposed to do. A madman had kidnapped Kendall and was taking her out of the country. And Graham was expected to sit quietly and listen.

"You're out of your mind," he said through clenched teeth.

"It would be a mistake for you to think so." Esteban leaned forward. The smile was gone, but the dark eyes still mocked him. "Braver men than you have tried to best me. Every last one of them is dead."

"What am I supposed to say to that?"

Esteban shrugged again. "You don't need to say anything. Your job at the moment is to listen, obey and remember the rules. Can you do that?"

Graham's hands were still trembling, but more now from helpless rage than fear. "Yes."

"Good. Because here is the last rule and it is by far the most important: break even one of the other rules and you will never see your wife again."

Moments ticked by before Graham said anything. When he spoke, he chose his words carefully. "How do I know she isn't already dead?"

Esteban's gaze met his. The brazen cruelty in his

dark eyes was chilling. "I'm afraid you'll have to take my word for it."

"Under the circumstances, I'm sure you can appreciate the difficulty I have in accepting your word for anything," Graham said bitterly. "I want to see her."

"Impossible." Esteban waved his hand as if swatting away a gnat. "As I said, she's on her way out of the country."

"Let me talk to her on the phone then."

Esteban's eyes turned even darker, colder as he continued to regard Graham. "I thought you understood the situation. It's very simple, *mi amigo*. If you want to see your wife again, you follow the rules."

"I think you're the one who has misunderstood the situation," Graham said coolly, but his heart bashed against his ribcage. "Unless you can prove to me that my wife is safe and unharmed, you won't get one red cent. Is that clear enough for you?"

For a moment, Graham thought that he'd gone too far. With one flicker of an eyelid, Gabriel Esteban could order his death, but Graham didn't care about his own safety. His only concern was for Kendall. He was no hero, but he instinctively knew that he had to make a stand here and now. Strength was the only thing a man like Esteban respected.

Esteban paused, then nodded, and the man standing nearest him produced a cell phone. Esteban punched in a number, barked a few orders in Spanish into the mouthpiece, then passed the phone to Graham.

He lifted it to his ear, not caring at the moment that Esteban and his men could see how badly his hands shook. "Kendall?"

There was a second of static and then he heard her sob his name. "Graham! Oh, God, I'm so sorry…"

"Don't. Just tell me you're okay."

"I'm…fine."

"Have they hurt you?"

The briefest of pauses. "No."

She was lying. He could hear the pain and fear in her voice, and the anger inside Graham deepened. He could feel the white-hot fury rushing through his veins, but for Kendall's sake, he had to remain calm.

"Stay strong," he told her. "I'm going to get us out of this. Do you hear me? Everything is going to be okay."

She was crying hard now and Graham heard her sob his name again a split second before the line went dead.

He handed the phone to Esteban. "Get her back. I need to tell her something."

"You'll have plenty of time to tell her anything you want just as long as you abide by the rules."

"Even if I follow the rules, what guarantee do I have that you'll release her? What would keep you from killing us both once you have the money?"

"My intention never was to kill your wife, Mr. Hollister." Esteban's voice was very soft, very deadly. "She's a beautiful woman. Worth far more to me alive than dead. Are you at all familiar with the black-market sex trade?"

Graham didn't think his fear or his fury could go any deeper, but he was wrong. The images racing through his head made him sick to his stomach, and it was all he could do not to go for Esteban's throat. At that moment, he could rip out the man's jugular with his bare hands.

But he wouldn't risk it. If he was injured—or worse, killed—and unable to meet the ransom demands, Graham now knew what was in store for Kendall.

Esteban folded his hands beneath his chin as he continued to regard Graham. "As you can see, the stakes are quite high. If you don't follow the rules, your wife will be sold to the highest bidder. No matter what happens tonight, her life will be spared. But I can promise you this—she'll soon be praying for death."

"Just tell me how much you want."

The smile came back. "I see we finally understand each other. That's good. That's progress." In one fluid movement, Esteban rose and stood staring down at Graham. "I think we've covered enough ground for tonight."

"What about the money?" Graham leaped to his feet. He wanted more than anything to have Esteban and his men out of his house, out of his life, but now it hit him that they were his only link to Kendall. "Tell me how much you want. We can end this tonight."

"I'm afraid it doesn't work that way. But don't worry. You'll be hearing from me again very soon." Esteban paused with another brief smile. "Please sit. There's really no need to see us out."

When Graham remained standing, Esteban lowered his voice. "Sit down, Mr. Hollister."

Graham hesitated, then dropped back down on the sofa without a word.

"I would advise you to take a few moments when you're alone to think about everything we've discussed tonight. Once my men and I are gone, you'll try very hard to come up with a way to extricate yourself and your wife from your current situation. You may even be tempted to call the police. That would be a very big mistake. My men will be watching you. Your house, your office, wherever you go. You won't be able to make a move that I won't know about. But in case you still don't appreciate the gravity of your situation, let me leave you with this."

He reached into his jacket pocket and pulled out a stack of photographs which he tossed one at a time onto the coffee table.

The first picture was of Graham's elderly grandmother in her hospital room. Graham's mother, Audrey, was seated next to her bed. The shot was clear and close enough that Graham could see the worry lines in his mother's face. Whoever took the picture had been standing only a few feet away.

The second photograph had been taken as Terrence and Ellie left the PemCo Tower earlier that night.

The third was a shot of Ashley getting into a car with some friends.

The fourth photograph was the most chilling of all. It was of five-year-old Caitlin and it had been taken through the window of her bedroom.

Graham's mouth went dry with fear as he glanced up. "You son of a bitch."

"As I said, I have no intention of killing your wife. She's much too valuable to sacrifice. But I have no such compunction when it comes to the rest of your family. With each rule that you break, someone you care about will die."

Esteban strode across the room to the shattered French doors. Pausing, he slowly turned back to Graham. "I would get this fixed if I were you. The damn coyotes…they get bolder all the time, do they not?"

Chapter Five

Graham remained seated for several minutes after Esteban and his men had left. He felt drugged, almost catatonic, yet thoughts rushed through his head at the speed of light and he couldn't seem to focus long enough to figure out what he should do first.

He stared at the photographs Esteban had spread across the coffee table. His whole family was in danger and he didn't know how in the hell to protect them.

His first instinct was to do as Esteban ordered. Stay put and wait for the first call. Do exactly as he was instructed. Follow the rules and everybody would get out of this alive.

But what if it wasn't that simple? What if the ransom demand was more than he could come up with in the amount of time he was given?

Mentally, he ran through his back accounts and stock holdings to see how much cash he could get his hands on quickly. The ransom would be sizeable. He had no doubt of that. Esteban wasn't some petty criminal. An operation like this must have been in the works for a long time.

Graham's earlier conversation with Ellie suddenly came back to him. Kendall had asked for a loan just last week. She'd needed a hundred thousand dollars for a reason that she felt she couldn't divulge to Ellie or to Graham. That amount of cash would mean nothing to a man like Esteban, and yet Graham couldn't help but think that Kendall's desperation for money was connected to her kidnapping. It was all tied together somehow.

And the ambassador's shooting? Was Esteban behind that as well?

The thought rocked Graham to the core because in the back of his mind, he'd been trying to convince himself that Esteban wasn't as dangerous as he wanted Graham to believe. The threat of killing off his family if he failed to play by the rules was just a way to keep him in line. Graham wanted desperately to believe it was all one big bluff.

But if Esteban had been responsible for the ambassador's shooting, if he had been willing to carry out an assassination attempt in a roomful of people, he wouldn't hesitate to go after Graham's family.

His gaze shot to the shattered French doors, and then he rose on shaky legs and walked out to the terrace to scan the grounds. He wasn't sure what he expected to see. If Esteban had left a lookout, darkness would shield him. But outside, away from the lights, Graham was hidden, too.

He headed away from the terrace, away from the pool lights, into the deeper shadows of the yard. He felt better out here, stronger, and for the first time since Esteban and his men had invaded his home, Graham's head began to clear. Even if the threat wasn't a bluff, there had to be a way out of this mess. He just had to think it through.

No matter how much he wanted to believe it was all a con, Graham knew the worst mistake he could make was to underestimate Gabriel Esteban. He'd seen the man's eyes. It wasn't hard to imagine that he was a cold-blooded killer who would do whatever it took to get what he wanted.

Graham turned slowly, scouring his surroundings. Then his gaze went back to the house. Even if Esteban didn't have anyone watching the place, the phone line could be tapped. He'd know if Graham made an outside call. His cell phone wasn't safe, either. Intercepting transmissions was a lot more difficult these days, but not impossible, nor was hacking into his e-mail account. The darkness in which he stood was nothing more than an illusion of cover, Graham realized. He was trapped, a prisoner in his own home.

His helplessness fueled his anger. His wife had been kidnapped, his family was in danger and he could do nothing but wait for Esteban's call. The man had him where he wanted him. Graham was doing precisely what Esteban would expect him to do.

And then it hit him. He'd been targeted for a reason. His personal wealth had been a factor, of course, but something else was at play here. Graham was a quiet, introspective man, not the type who would be expected to resort to physical retaliation. He would undoubtedly strike a man like Gabriel Esteban as being weak and controllable. An easy mark. A man who would do exactly as he was told.

The rage twisted in Graham's gut like a red-hot poker. The night was mild, but beneath his tux, he was sweating and he stripped off his jacket, tossing it onto a lounger as he walked across the pool deck and headed for the house.

A few minutes later, he came back out, this time dressed in jeans, a dark shirt and sneakers. Myron was sitting in the courtyard cleaning a front paw. He cried for some attention, but all Graham had time to do was give him a brief pat on the head as he let him in. Besides, it was Kendall that Myron wanted, not Graham.

He'd left Esteban's phone inside the house. As long as it was turned on and in his possession, he could be tracked. But leaving it behind could be even more dangerous. If Esteban called and Graham didn't answer, the second rule would be broken. He was taking a terrible risk with his family's safety, but if Esteban had targeted Graham because he thought he could control him, his arrogance might lead him to believe that his rules wouldn't be challenged.

It was a gamble and the stakes couldn't have been higher, but Graham could no longer sit around impotently weighing his options. He needed to act quickly in order to catch Esteban off guard.

Graham hurried through the darkness, hitting the path to the creek at some point just beyond the pool. As he neared the rushing water, he turned right, cutting through the wooded grounds to the fence that surrounded his property.

Half a mile down the road was a convenience store and gas station that he sometimes stopped at for coffee and to fill up on his way into work in the mornings. There were pay phones outside the store. Most everyone used cell phones these days, so whether any of them still worked, he had no idea. But he would find out soon enough.

Driving to the store would have saved precious time, but if Esteban had left surveillance behind, the car would be spotted before it ever left the premises. Graham would be followed and within a matter of minutes, Esteban would know that he had made outside contact.

Graham was besieged by second thoughts. Was he doing the right thing? He couldn't know, of course. He'd never faced anything remotely like the situation in which he now found himself. And Esteban was counting on that.

But even if he followed the rules, if he sat back and did nothing until Esteban called, how could he be sure the man would keep his word? That his family would be safe and Kendall would be freed?

Once Esteban had the money, he could simply disappear across the border and she would be at his mercy. He would get away with it, too, so long as he had Graham's cooperation. He was banking on that, too, and on Graham's desperation to protect his family.

He *was* desperate. But he also knew that it would be stupid and naive to try and go this alone. He had to have help and the sooner the better.

FIVE MINUTES later he had the convenience store in sight. He stayed in the shadows and watched the road for several seconds before crossing to the other side.

It occurred to him as he sprinted across the lighted parking lot that if Esteban was as intent on watching his every move as he'd said, he might have the convenience store staked out. The proximity to Graham's house made it the logical place for him to try and contact the authorities without anyone's knowledge.

But it was a little too late to turn back now. Graham had made up his mind, and as he approached the nearest phone and lifted the receiver to check for a dial tone, he turned slightly so that he could scan the parking lot and road behind him. The area looked deserted, and from where he stood, he could also see inside the store. The clerk sat behind the counter reading a book and didn't look up. If anyone else was about, he was too well-hidden for Graham to detect.

Fishing Delacourt's card from his pocket along with his credit card, Graham quickly placed the call, turning now to shield his face from the road.

The phone rang twice before it engaged on the other end.

"Delacourt." It was after two o'clock in the morning, but the special agent sounded as fresh and alert as if it were mid-day.

"This is Graham Hollister. We spoke earlier in Houston. I'm the architect—"

"I know who you are, Mr. Hollister. I assume the reason you're calling at this hour is because you've remembered something."

Graham wiped a trickle of sweat from his brow with his forearm. "That's not why I'm calling. I need your help with something."

"I'm listening." Delacourt spoke in a deliberate tone. He gave away nothing of what he might be thinking.

"I'm in trouble," Graham blurted as his heart hammered against his chest.

Delacourt's hesitation was almost infinitesimal. "What kind of trouble?"

For a moment, as Graham's chest threatened to crack, he couldn't say a word. Emotion welled in his throat and he felt as if he'd been hit head-on by a speeding bus.

"Mr. Hollister?"

"I'm still here." He cleared his throat and mopped his face. "What I'm about to tell you…" He ran out of words again, this time not so much from shock and nerves, but because he literally didn't know where or how to start. It still seemed unreal to him; the danger hanging over his family nothing more than a remnant of a terrible nightmare.

But it *was* real. And until he found a way to stop a madman, everyone he cared about remained vulnerable.

"Earlier tonight four armed men broke into my home in Austin. They told me they've kidnapped my wife and unless I do exactly as they say, I'll never see her again."

"How long ago did this happen?" Delacourt's voice altered only slightly, but Graham knew the agent was now listening intently to his every word.

"About an hour ago. Maybe a little longer. I think they're still watching my house to make sure I don't go to the police. That's why I'm using a pay phone. I was afraid they could monitor my landline and cell phone."

"How long since you've seen your wife?"

"Since she left the reception earlier tonight."

"But you said you talked to her on the phone."

"I did, but I think they had her even then. She said some things that didn't make sense. I think she was under duress."

"So the threat seems credible to you."

Graham squeezed his eyes closed. "Yes. I was told that she's being taken out of the country and unless I do as I'm told, she'll be sold to the highest bidder. I was also given a list of rules and for every one I break, someone in my family will die…" He trailed off, the impact of his decision to call in the authorities hitting him full force. He started to tremble. "If they find out I've called you—"

"Just take it easy. You did the right thing. Too many people make the mistake of not bringing us in soon enough. Those cases almost never end well. You did the right thing," Delacourt stressed. "Now tell me the rest."

Graham wiped the back of his hand across his mouth. "He showed me photographs of my mother and grandmother, my brother and his family…all of them taken within the last few hours. They were somehow able to get that close. They even had a shot of my five-year-old niece taken through her bedroom window." He felt sick to his stomach when he thought about how close they'd been to Caitlin. What kind of man would threaten an innocent child?

The answer was obvious and devastating. A cold, brutal psychopath, a man without a shred of remorse or conscience.

"You must see this sort of thing all the time." Graham leaned his forehead against the kiosk. "Do you think it's at all possible this could be one big bluff? Maybe they just wanted to frighten me so that I'd give them what they want."

The FBI agent took his time answering, and his silence filled Graham with dread. But it was what he already knew in his heart to be true. He'd been grasping at straws, hoping against hope that his family was in no real danger. But that wasn't the case.

"Anytime there's a ransom demand with death threats, we have to go on the assumption that the kidnappers mean what they say. What did they ask for?"

"Nothing specific yet. I was given a phone and told to keep it with me at all times. They'd be in touch."

"Do you have the phone with you now?"

Graham hesitated, wondering what Delacourt would think of his decision to leave it behind. "No."

"Good. As long as it's turned on, they can track you."

"I know that. But I can't stay away much longer. I have to get back in case he calls."

"I understand, but I'm going to need a few more details. You said the demands weren't specific. What did you mean by that?"

"Just what I said. I was told there would be several ransom drops, each to be arranged at a future time, and there would be other things they would need from me besides money."

"What can you tell me about the ringleader, the

guy who did all the talking? Can you give me a description?"

"I can do better than that. I can tell you his name. Gabriel Esteban. He's tall. I'd say at least six feet and thin, wiry. Well-dressed and well-spoken. He's probably in his late forties to early fifties, and he has acne scars on his face. He spoke with an accent. I think it was Mexican."

"I doubt that he gave you his real name," Delacourt said. "And I doubt that we'll find anyone meeting his description on our watch list. The fact that he let you see him so clearly means he's not afraid of being identified."

"I thought it meant that he plans to kill me," Graham said.

"We'll do everything in our power to make sure that doesn't happen," Delacourt said. "What about the others?"

"They all wore ski masks."

"Which means they *were* concerned about being identified," the agent mused. "Tell me exactly when you last saw your wife."

Graham glanced over his shoulder. The road was still clear behind him. "I already told you, it was at the reception. I saw her speak to someone when she came in to the room. A man. The next time I saw her she was at the door."

Delacourt's voice sharpened. "You didn't mention this man earlier when we spoke."

"I didn't think it was important. As I said, I saw her leave the room. She didn't look frightened. I had no reason to believe she wasn't leaving of her own accord."

"Did you recognize the man she spoke to?"

"No. I'd never seen him before. But I think Kendall knew him. I think he somehow coerced her into leaving the reception and then Esteban's men grabbed her outside the building."

"Can you describe this guy?"

"Hispanic. Tall and thin like Esteban, but younger. My age maybe. Mid-thirties."

"It would have been helpful if you'd told us about him earlier. I'm still wondering why you didn't."

Desperation seeped into Graham's voice. "Look, I thought this was something personal. I didn't see a need to bring it up. I had no way of knowing my wife was about to be kidnapped."

"Tell me about the phone call you received. You said she sounded under duress."

"She asked me to meet her at home, in Austin. I thought it was strange because we'd planned to spend the night in Houston. Now I realize that someone told her what to say." A car went by without slowing. Graham turned to watch the taillights.

"Which probably means they were in a hurry to get out of Houston. They felt safer dealing with you in Austin."

"Do you think my wife's kidnapping is connected to the shooting?"

"The timing is suspicious. And demands other than monetary are not the sort of thing we hear in kidnappings for ransom."

Graham's hand tightened on the phone. What the hell was going on here? How had he and Kendall become enmeshed in an assassination attempt? It didn't make sense. Nothing that had happened in the last several hours made any sense.

He drew a long breath. "Look, whether they're connected or not…I need you to help me get my wife back. I need you to find Gabriel Esteban before he hurts my family."

"We can put your family under surveillance," Delacourt said. "They'll be protected. We have agents who are expert in dealing with kidnappings and hostage situations. I'll need to send a team up to see you as soon as I can arrange it."

"You said we have to go on the assumption that Esteban means what he says. He said that my house would be under surveillance, my every move watched by his men. If strange cars start pulling up in my driveway, he'll know that I've called the authorities."

"We know how to handle these kinds of situations."

"How?"

"You'll just have to trust me."

"That's not good enough," Graham said as he shot another look toward the street. "I've thought of something that might work. Esteban's men broke through glass doors to enter my home. He mentioned when he left that I should get them fixed. To keep out the coyotes, he said. Maybe you could somehow use that as a cover."

Graham had expected Delacourt to scoff at the idea, to tell him he'd been watching too many James Bond movies. But instead, the agent said tersely, "Hold on."

A few seconds later, Delacourt was back on the line. "When you get back home, call Hill Country Windows and Doors on IH35. They have a twenty-four-hour emergency service. Ask them to come within the hour."

"What if they can't make it that soon?"

"They will. I'll arrange everything from this end. All you need to do is make the call. And Mr. Hollister?"

"Yes?"

"Try to stay calm. I know this is a difficult situation, but you did the right thing by calling us in. The FBI has a very successful recovery rate in kidnappings for ransom."

"And if this is no ordinary kidnapping for ransom?"

"Let's take it one step at a time."

Graham's hands were still shaking as he hung up, and in spite of Delacourt's words of encouragement, he could no longer fight the terror crawling through his veins.

Esteban wanted something besides money. And in order to free Kendall and keep the rest of his family safe, Graham would have to meet his demands.

No matter what he had to do.

LESS THAN an hour later, a white panel van with the glass company's logo on the side pulled up in front of the house. A man dressed in jeans and a baseball cap got out and came to the door. He played it so straight that Graham had no idea if he was a federal agent or a glass repairman.

He instructed the man to pull the van around back between the courtyard and pool where they would have easy access to the broken doors. The walled courtyard would also serve as a screen to hide them from anyone watching the house.

Graham stood in the courtyard as five men piled out of the van and began to unload the equipment. One of them approached him and motioned for him to follow him over to the van. They stood at the back, pretending to examine the new set of doors.

"I'm Special Agent Dean Heller." He was a young-looking guy, about Graham's age, with short, blond hair and a pleasant, angular face. He didn't fit the stereotypical image of a federal agent, nor did his easygoing demeanor inspire the kind of confidence Graham had been hoping for.

"The man in the baseball cap is Special Agent Andy Pinson. He and Agent Jones—the tall guy— are here to sweep for bugs and wire taps, that sort of thing. You'll need to show them around, let them get a feel for the place. When we're through, Agent Jones will stay behind to monitor the operation from this end." Casually, he pointed to something inside the van. "The other two guys are here to fix your doors. Any questions?"

Graham had plenty of those. "What happens if your men find something?"

The agent leaned into the van and adjusted a piece of equipment. "That's something we need to talk about right now. If we find and remove any listening devices, they'll know—at the very least—that you've brought someone in to sweep for bugs. But leaving the damn things in place can also be risky because they'll hear everything that is said and done inside your house. That means you can't slip. You may be tempted to ask Jones a question or say something to him without thinking. You can't do that. You'll have to act as if you're alone, and that can be a lot harder than it sounds. One mistake and they're onto us."

"I don't see how we have a choice," Graham said. "If we remove the bugs, Esteban could retaliate against my family."

"We're taking care of your family. We'll have them watched around the clock."

But Graham was worried. Very worried. However, his initial assessment of Heller was changing. He appreciated the fact that the agent had immediately brought him into the operation and asked for his opinion rather than keeping him in the dark.

They went inside and Graham gave Pinson and Jones a quick tour of the house and they set to work. They started with Graham's office and once they gave Heller the all-clear sign, he motioned for Graham to follow him inside and closed the door.

Heller nodded toward Graham's desk. "Do you mind?"

Before Graham could answer, the agent walked around the desk and sat down, then waved Graham toward a leather chair positioned just to his right. "Have a seat."

Graham was too keyed up to sit, but as his gaze met Heller's, he realized the agent's laid-back attitude had vanished. There was something in his eyes now. Maybe not suspicion, but a wary glint that caught Graham off guard.

"Please have a seat, Mr. Hollister. This could take some time and you may as well be comfortable. We have a lot to go over."

Whether he realized it or not, his command was almost identical to the one Esteban had issued earlier that night. The similarity annoyed and angered Graham because he was damn tired of being jerked around.

But at the moment, he had little choice but to do as the agent said. He'd called in the FBI because he knew he couldn't find Kendall on his own. Now the feds were in control and he had to do as they advised because his only hope at the moment came from Delacourt's earlier assurance that they knew what they were doing. And they had a high percentage of successful recoveries.

Graham took a seat, but he was far from relaxed.

He felt restless and anxious for action rather than more questions.

He stared at Heller across the desk. "Can you find my wife?" he asked bluntly.

"We're going to do everything in our power to bring her home safely. You have my word on that. But we can't do it without your full cooperation. I need to ask you a lot of questions. You won't understand the purpose of some of them. You may be embarrassed or uncomfortable at times, maybe even angry. But it's imperative that you answer truthfully."

Graham nodded. "What is it you want to know?"

"I need to hear everything that led up to your wife's departure from the reception and your subsequent encounter with the alleged kidnappers—"

"What do you mean alleged?"

Heller smiled and the mellow disposition surfaced briefly. "Don't be alarmed by the language. We're highly trained in ambiguity."

"I'll try to remember that," Graham muttered.

Heller pulled a file folder from a briefcase on the desk that Graham hadn't even noticed until now. He watched curiously as Heller took out a small recorder and held it up. "Do you have any objections?"

"No, that's fine."

"As I said, I'll want you to recount the events leading up to your wife's disappearance, but first I need to establish some background information."

"Whatever you need."

"I appreciate your attitude." Heller paused to turn on the tape recorder, then prefaced the interview by stating his name, Graham's name, the date and their location into the mike. Then he placed the tiny machine on the desk between them.

"How long have you and your wife been married, Mr. Hollister?"

The question took Graham by surprise. "We were married seven years ago in Vegas, but we separated a few months later. We reconciled five years ago.

"Right after your wife's accident in Mexico."

Graham blinked. "Yes, that's right."

"Kendall Hollister worked in Mexico during the separation, didn't she?"

"Yes."

"Did you have much contact with her while you were apart?"

Graham shifted uneasily. This was beginning to sound more like a cross-examination than an interview. "No, not really. I was living in California at the time. We exchanged an occasional phone call or e-mail."

"Did she tell you anything about the company she worked for?"

"No. I didn't even know she'd moved to Mexico until a friend told me."

"She worked for a man named Leo Kittering. Have you ever heard her mention him?"

Graham shook his head, then caught himself and said, "No, never."

Heller studied him for a moment. "Kittering is an American citizen who has lived in Mexico for the past thirty years. He fled across the border after being charged with some serious crimes here in the States, extortion being one of them."

Graham swallowed painfully. "You think he's connected to the kidnapping?"

"That's what we're trying to find out, but it's not easy dealing with a guy like Kittering. He remarried several years ago and his second wife's family is well-connected. He's used their money and influence to build himself an empire. He's virtually untouchable."

"So what do we do?"

"We keep digging for now. A guy like Kittering has enemies, and some of them may be persuaded to talk."

"You said he has an empire. What does he do?"

"He has a number of interests, but most of his holdings are a front for his real business."

"Which is?""

"He runs one of the largest drug cartels in Mexico."

Graham couldn't hide his shock. "Kendall couldn't have known about that when she worked for him. She wouldn't be party to something like that."

"You hadn't known your wife long when the two of you married, right? And a few months after the Vegas ceremony, you separated. You said yourself you had very little contact with her during that time.

You can't be all that certain of what she was or wasn't involved in, can you?"

Graham's hands tightened on the arms of his chair. "I know my wife. I know she would never be mixed up in what you're suggesting." His gaze hardened as he stared at Heller across the desk. "And what the hell does any of this have to do with Kendall's kidnapping? Why are you trying to dig up personal dirt on my wife when you should be focusing on trying to find her?"

Heller let him finish before he said calmly, "As I said earlier, we're doing everything in our power to find your wife and bring her home safely. Her connection to Leo Kittering may not have anything to do with her kidnapping, but at this stage of the game, we can't afford to overlook any possibility."

"How did you dig this stuff up so quickly? How did you even know about our separation?" Graham asked.

"Let's just say, the events of the evening brought certain facts to light in our database searches."

"In other words, you were already doing a background check on me," Graham said. "Why?"

"A high-level foreign diplomat was shot on American soil. You can be sure we're looking closely at everyone who was at that reception."

"But all these questions about Kendall and our separation. It sounds to me as if you think we're guilty of something."

"I'm just trying to do my job, Mr. Hollister."

Graham scrubbed a hand across his face. This whole meeting was leaving a very bad taste in his mouth, and he was having second thoughts about calling in the FBI.

"Are you ready to continue?" Heller pressed.

Graham's gaze met his. "I don't know. Maybe I need to get a lawyer over here first."

Heller shrugged. "That's your prerogative, of course. But you'd be wasting valuable time. And there might be some who'd wonder why you feel you need one."

Graham leaped to his feet. "And I can't help wondering why you're not already out there looking for my wife instead of wasting valuable time with all these asinine questions. I'm starting to wonder if you people even know what the hell you're doing."

"You need to calm down," Heller told him firmly. "My line of questioning may not make sense to you, but I assure you there's a purpose behind everything we're doing. We're in this together, Mr. Hollister. The more information you can provide, the more we have to go on. It's as simple as that. Without your cooperation, our hands are tied. Now do we continue or not?"

Their gazes met again across the desk, and Graham finally nodded. He sat back down and answered the rest of Heller's questions. Because, like it or not, the FBI was the best chance he had of finding Kendall.

Chapter Six

A little while later, Heller informed Graham that they'd found nothing in the sweep. The house and phone lines were clean, and though Graham felt somewhat relieved by the news, he knew there were other ways to monitor his movements. Heller warned him—and Graham agreed—that they still had to proceed with the assumption that Esteban meant what he said.

"So what do we do now?" Graham asked anxiously.

"We sit tight and wait. And I can tell you from experience that this phase is the hardest part. You'll be so wired by the time the call finally comes in that you could easily make a mistake. Don't let that happen. Use this time to rest and stay focused."

Graham jammed his hands into his pockets as he watched the agents repack the sensitive equipment. "What about my family? Shouldn't I at least alert them of the danger? It doesn't seem right leaving them in the dark."

"It may not seem right, but that's exactly what you

have to do," Heller said. "A change in their routine or behavior could put them at even greater risk. Believe me when I tell you that every precaution is being taken to safeguard your family. They're under constant surveillance. No one will get near them that we don't know about."

Graham wished he could take the agent at his word, but the tone of Heller's earlier interrogation had eroded his confidence and trust. Graham wasn't at all certain that keeping his family in the dark was the best way to protect them, nor was he convinced, at this point, that the FBI had his best interests at heart. The grilling had left him uneasy.

After the van had been loaded, everyone cleared out except for Special Agent Jones. Graham was exhausted, but he knew he wouldn't be able to sleep. He couldn't even sit still. His mind raced with every conceivable scenario, and the smallest noise caused him to start. Every tick of the clock became an excruciating measure of his desperation.

It didn't take long to realize that Heller was right. The waiting was the hardest part.

Graham prowled the house, finally stopping at a window in the living room where he could stare out at the darkness. It would be dawn soon. The beginning of the first day. How long would it before Esteban called with a demand?

Behind him, he could hear Special Agent Jones rechecking the equipment that would allow him to track and record incoming calls. Graham hadn't said anything as he'd watched the agent set up, but he'd thought to himself that the effort was futile. Esteban wouldn't be foolish enough to call on a landline. He'd left a phone for a reason—a cell call was a lot harder to trace despite how easy Hollywood made it look.

Triangulating the source depended on the strength, angle and timing of the signal measured at two or more towers. And Esteban was smart enough to take the added precautions of using talk-and-toss phones, routers, calls made from different locations using multiple servers. For all any of them knew, the ransom calls to Graham would be placed from out of the country. Pinpointing a location would be like looking for a needle in a haystack.

"You might want to reconsider catching a little shut-eye," Jones finally said.

"It's not exactly a conscious decision," Graham said with a frown. "There's just no way I can sleep right now."

"Sometimes it *is* a conscious decision. Think of those guys who learned to sleep in muddy trenches with bullets flying overhead. At least you've got a nice soft bed waiting for you."

Graham didn't say anything as he continued to watch the darkness.

"Look, I know this isn't easy. You're worried sick about your family. I get that. But you've been through a lot tonight and the next few days are only going to get tougher. You may have to make split-second decisions that could affect your family's lives, so you'll need to stay sharp and focused. You'd better get some rest now while you can."

"Are you married, Agent Jones?"

He hesitated, then said almost sheepishly, "I'm a newlywed. I've only been married a few months."

"Congratulations." Graham glanced over his shoulder. "If it was your wife out there somewhere, would you be able to sleep?"

"No, probably not," he admitted. "I imagine I'd be doing exactly what you are. And when that first call came in, I'd probably be so exhausted and stressed, I'd be apt to make a lot of foolish mistakes. You don't want that to happen."

"Have you worked kidnapping cases before?"

"More than a few."

"How did they end?"

Another hesitation. "Every case is different. I'm not going to lie to you. They don't always end the way we want them to. But we're good at what we do, Mr. Hollister. You have to trust that."

"I don't really have a choice, do I?" Graham turned back to the window. "How long have you been with the FBI?"

"Ten years. They recruited me during my senior year at M.I.T."

"M.I.T.?" Graham was surprised. "I thought they went after lawyers and psychologists."

"Oh, we've got plenty of those in the Bureau," Jones said dryly. "Lawyers and shrinks. Gotta be a bus joke in there somewhere, right?"

Graham smiled slightly. "I'll bet Agent Heller was a lawyer in his other life. I'm guessing a prosecutor."

Jones grinned. "What gave it away?"

"His interviewing technique leaves a lot to be desired."

"So I've been told." The amusement faded in the agent's voice. "Be that as it may, he's one of the best agents I've ever worked with. You're lucky to have him on this case. He doesn't get sidetracked and he never gives up. That's what you want on something like this."

"What do you mean, on something like this?"

"From what you've told us, the kidnappers don't plan to wrap things up with one drop. Esteban said there'd be more than one ransom demand, and he has other things he wants from you besides money. If this turns out to be a protracted situation, you want a bulldog like Heller on your team."

A protracted situation. *Dear God.*

Graham swallowed. "How long does a resolution usually take?"

"Like I said, every case is different. Could be a matter of hours or it could take weeks. We don't know what we're dealing with yet. But if I were you, I'd prepare myself for the long haul, which means you need to grab some sleep while you still can.

When that first call comes in, you may be tested in ways you've yet to imagine."

Graham didn't feel like arguing the point so he nodded and left the room. He went into the kitchen and put food in Myron's bowl, gave him some fresh water, and then walked down the hall to the bedroom and stepped inside.

Leaning against the door, he closed his eyes as Jones's warning rang in his ears.

You may have to make split-second decisions that could affect your family's lives....

Graham could feel the cold terror clawing at his throat, pushing him closer and closer to desperation.

You may be tested in ways you've yet to imagine.

What the hell did Esteban have in mind for him? And what if he wasn't up to the challenge? What if his family was killed off one by one because he couldn't meet Esteban's demands?

How would he live with himself if anything happened to his family? Especially to his nieces. They were just children. They had their whole lives ahead of them. His mother and grandmother, Terrence and Ellie…he couldn't lose any of them. Whatever it took, he had to protect them.

And Kendall…he had to get her back. He had to bring her home safely. No other option could even be considered.

Yet as Graham stood with his back to the door, terrible thoughts rushed through his head. He wished he could crawl into bed, pull the covers over his head and make it all disappear.

But his life was never going to be that simple again, and he had a bad feeling that things were going to get a lot worse before they got better. He kept thinking about the term Jones had used—*a protracted situation*. It could be days or even weeks before they had a resolution, and at the moment, Graham wasn't certain how he would make it through the next few hours.

Pushing himself away from the door, he went into the bathroom, stripped off all his clothes and climbed into the shower. But he kept thinking he heard the phone, so he got back out, dried off and carried Esteban's phone into the bedroom where he quickly dressed in jeans and a T-shirt and lay down on top of the bed. He placed the phone on his nightstand next to a picture of Kendall.

Curling one arm beneath his head, he picked up the frame in his free hand and studied her face, his eyes dry and burning with emotion.

It was a recent shot, but not a clear one. Kendall had her face turned away from the camera and he'd caught her in profile. That happened a lot. Since the accident, she wasn't crazy about having her picture taken, but she didn't like having the old photographs around, either. For the longest time, she hadn't been able to look at them. She'd once been a stunningly gorgeous woman and adjusting to her altered appearance had been difficult for her. Was still difficult for her.

Graham thought her beautiful, more so now than ever because she had a radiance about her that hadn't been there before. When she looked at him, her eyes glowing and her lips slightly parted in that enticing way she had…

When she reached for him in the middle of the night…

Whispered how much she loved him…wanted him…

Graham's chest ached as memories threatened to crush him. When he'd first seen Kendall in Mexico after the accident, she'd still been swathed in bandages. Even though the doctors had tried to prepare him for how badly her face had been damaged, he hadn't been able to fathom the extent of her injuries until he'd seen her. Even then, hidden as she'd been by the gauze, he'd been able to mask his emotions.

It wasn't until days later, after the first surgery, when the bandages had been removed, that reality had hit him like a fist between the eyes. He'd been so stunned he hadn't been able to hide his shock.

After that, Kendall wouldn't let him look at her again. Whenever he came to visit, she made sure the lights in her room were lowered. Or she would sit in shadows, her face turned away from him.

After the fourth surgery, Graham had begun to glimpse hints of the old Kendall. By this time they were back in Houston, and the surgeon who performed the procedure was world-renowned for his advancements in reconstructive techniques.

Once the swelling went down, the result had been amazing. Kendall was never going to be as outwardly beautiful as she'd been before the accident, but her appearance hadn't mattered to Graham. He'd fallen in love with her all over again, but it had taken a long time to convince her that his feelings were genuine.

When he'd asked her to renew their vows, she'd been hesitant and wary. "Why do you want to do this?"

"Because the first time we exchanged vows was for all the wrong reasons. We hurried into something neither of us was ready for, but it's different now. I want us to make a commitment to each other for the right reasons this time."

She closed her eyes. "Are you sure about this? You don't just…feel sorry for me?"

"Why would I feel sorry for you? The doctor said you're on the road to making a full recovery."

"My face…"

"I love your face."

"You know something?" She looked deeply into his eyes. "I almost believe you really mean that."

"I love you, Kendall. I want us to spend the rest of our lives together."

"Then I'll marry you," she said softly. "As many times as you want me to."

His family hadn't been as supportive of the reunion as he'd hoped. His mother and brother had never really warmed up to Kendall, and Graham suspected they'd both been relieved when she left him. News of their reconciliation hadn't thrilled either of them, but it was Michael's reaction that surprised Graham the most. He'd seemed almost angry by the news.

"Don't do it. You'd be making the second biggest mistake of your life. A woman like that—"

"A woman like what?" His tone warned Michael to watch what he said.

Michael sighed. "Look, you're a good guy, Graham, and you feel obligated to see her through this. I understand that. But let's face it, you were headed for a divorce before the accident. All the problems you had before are still there. They've just been temporarily swept aside."

"You're wrong. We're not the same people we were before. We've both had our eyes opened to what's really important."

"It may seem that way now—"

"It *is* that way. I'm in love with her, Michael. I don't understand why you and everyone else can't be happy for us."

Michael hesitated, as if on the verge of arguing further. Then he shrugged and looked away. "Hey, if this is really what you want, then you have my blessing. I'll even give the bride away. Better yet, I'll host the party at my place."

The complete one-eighty took Graham by surprise. "You don't have to go that far."

"If you're going to do this, then I want to be a part of it. I've got a great big house with a gorgeous garden and no one to enjoy it. I've been thinking about putting it on the market. Trish is the one who wanted that place. Now that she's moved out…" He shrugged again and changed the subject.

Like Terrence and Ellie, Michael and his ex-wife, Trish, had been high-school sweethearts. They'd always seemed so much in love, the perfect couple, so it was a shock to Graham when they separated and quickly divorced while he was in L.A.

Michael never volunteered the reason behind the breakup and Graham hadn't pushed. At the time, he'd had his own messy personal life to worry about. But he wondered if Michael's disappointment in his own failed marriage contributed to his reservations over Graham and Kendall's reconciliation.

The phone on the nightstand rang, dragging him back to the present, and Graham reached for it, swinging his legs over the side of the bed as he answered.

"Hello?"

"Check your e-mail, Mr. Hollister."

"Wait—"

But the caller had already hung up.

Graham got up and went into the hallway, calling out to Jones as he hurried into his office. The agent followed a moment later.

"A call came in," Graham said. "He told me to check my e-mail. Then he hung up."

Graham was seated behind his desk and he quickly logged onto his e-mail account. He scrolled down the list until he found the subject line he wanted: *Kendall*.

His hand was clammy on the mouse as he opened the e-mail. Inside he clicked on a hyperlink that took him to a live Webcam site with streaming video.

At first, he didn't know what he was looking at. The feed was grainy and the room in which the camera was mounted almost completely dark. Then suddenly a light came on, and Graham saw a woman lying on a narrow cot that was shoved up against one wall. Her back was to the camera, but he knew it was Kendall.

He sucked in a sharp breath, the pain in his chest as sharp as a knife thrust.

As he watched, she rolled over and sat up, her gaze on something across the room that Graham couldn't see. From her expression and the direction of her gaze, he thought someone must have come into the room. He even thought he saw her lips move, but there was no audio and the feed was too poor to be sure.

Slowly, her head turned toward the camera, and for just a split second, he caught a glimpse of her face. She still had on the red dress she'd worn to the reception, but her shoes were missing. She looked scared to death as she wrapped her arms around her middle and turned away from the camera.

As he continued to watch, she jumped and cringed,

as if a loud noise had startled her, and then a moment later, a man came into view. Graham saw nothing but his back, but he could tell the newcomer was large with thick, black hair curling over the collar of his shirt.

He reached down and jerked Kendall to her feet. Her eyes went wide with fear as her hand flew up to her face. But she was too late to fend off the blow. He struck her hard with the back of his hand and she stumbled back. Her legs buckled and she sprawled onto the cot, cowering away from her attacker.

Still keeping his back to the camera, the man disappeared. Kendall curled her knees into her chest as one hand cradled her wounded cheek. Graham couldn't see her face. He had no idea how badly she was hurt.

All he knew was how much he wanted to kill the son of a bitch who had hit her.

His hands tightened into fists.

He'd never thought of himself as a violent man, but at that moment he had no doubt he could easily take a life without one iota of remorse.

He swore viciously into the silence.

"Take it easy," Jones warned him. "That's exactly the reaction they want from you. They're trying to keep you off guard and vulnerable."

Graham glanced away, trying to compose his emotions. He was holding onto his control by a thread. He needed to hit something. Anything. He needed to assuage the murderous rage spiraling through him before he did something he'd live to regret.

"I know it's hard to watch something like that," Jones said, "but he didn't really hurt her. Focus on that. She actually looks in much better shape than I'd expected."

Graham barely heard him. His eyes remained glued to the screen. He kept hoping that Kendall would turn back to the camera so that he could know she was okay. The brief glimpse he'd had of her face wasn't enough. But she remained exactly where she was, and a moment later, they lost the feed.

Even after the screen went blank, Graham couldn't tear his gaze away. He couldn't move. His senses were shutting down and he couldn't seem to focus on anything but the computer screen.

"See if you can get the feed back," the agent coaxed.

Graham hit the link again, but it was dead.

The feed was gone.

Graham didn't know how long he'd been staring at the screen when Jones finally said, "We've got some work to do. My guess is they're going through a router, probably more than one, but we need to find out for sure."

Slowly Graham stood and let the agent have his place in front of the computer. Jones was already on the phone, and Graham listened for a moment before he turned and left the office.

He walked down the hallway, out the newly repaired French doors and sat down at the wrought-iron table in the courtyard. The sky glowed faintly on the horizon, and a gray light settled like mist over the landscape. He could smell the jasmine and honeysuckle that spilled over the walls of the courtyard, and the scent filled him with a terrible longing.

He wanted to turn back the clock. Just twenty-four hours ago, he'd been on top of the world. Secure in his marriage, happy in his career. A man who wanted for nothing.

And now, one day later, everything had changed. *He* had changed. Just a few short hours ago, he would never have thought himself capable of taking a life, and yet he knew that he could do so now without a second thought. It wasn't hard to imagine his hands wrapped around the thick neck of the man who had struck Kendall, squeezing and squeezing until the last breath of life had been forced from the man's lungs.

Esteban had warned him that life as he knew it was over. Graham understood that now. No matter the outcome, there would be no going back to the way things were before, to the man he'd once been. That was all gone.

And if it took him the rest of his life, he would hunt down Gabriel Esteban and make him pay for what he had done.

SOMEHOW Kendall had managed to doze off. Her eyes snapped open, though, as the door opened with a creak, and she drew herself up, cringing in anticipation of what was to come.

At this point, she had no idea how long she'd been locked up. It seemed like days, but she knew that it had only been a matter of hours. After she'd gotten into the van with Hector Reyes, she'd been driven out of the city to a small, clandestine landing strip used, she imagined, in the drug trade.

She'd been blindfolded, handcuffed and transferred to a private plane that had taken off moments later. She had no idea who else was on board besides the pilot. No one said anything. She tried to calculate the direction and flying time, but the blindfold disoriented her and her fear made it impossible to concentrate.

Finally, they'd landed and she'd been put in the back of a car. A short while later, she'd been shoved into this small, damp room. Only then had the cuffs and blindfold been removed, and she'd been left alone in the dark with only her outstretched hands to guide her around the cramped space.

They'd taken her shoes and the first thing she noticed was the rough texture of the floor. It felt like an old concrete slab that had chipped and cracked over the years. The walls were cinder block, the only furnishing, a single cot placed against one wall.

Earlier, when the light had come on briefly, she'd had a better look and noticed with relief that the room had a sink and toilet behind a tattered curtain. The fixtures were old and worn, but fairly clean.

A camera had been mounted on one of the walls.

Kendall had been instructed to look straight up at the lens, to turn her head so that the bruises on her face could be seen. That was when she knew that Graham must have been watching, so that he could see what they'd done to her. That was why she'd refused to do as they asked. She didn't want him seeing her like this.

The man had struck her again, not because of her refusal, but because they wanted Graham to witness their brutality firsthand. They wanted his imagination to run wild, wanted to shake him up so badly he'd do whatever they asked of him.

And now someone had come back to the room, and Kendall shivered, remembering the way the man earlier had looked at her. She still wore the dress she'd had on at the reception, and she felt exposed and vulnerable. She wished she could cover up, but there were no linens on the cot. Just a thin, worn mattress that had seen only God knew what kind of use.

As the door opened, weak sunlight filtered into the room and Kendall blinked. It was morning. The first day of her captivity.

Her gaze was riveted to the opening, not in anticipation of who would step through, but because the sunshine was like a beacon, a ray of hope. Graham had said on the phone that he would find a way to get them out of this mess. Somehow he would come for her and everything would be okay. They could go back to their lives, go back to their dreams and happiness. Kendall desperately needed to believe that.

But a part of her already knew that her old life—her *new* old life—was gone forever. The secrets and lies had finally caught up with her.

A young woman entered the door carrying a tray. She walked quickly across the room, head down, and placed the tray on the floor near the cot. Then she started to back away.

"No, wait!" Kendall got up off the cot. "Tell me where I am. What's going to happen to me?"

The woman's head lifted and Kendall gasped. "I know you. Your name is Maria. You're Hector's sister."

The woman's gaze shot to the door, then she said softly in Spanish, "*Por favor.* Just do as they say. You won't be harmed."

Her gentle voice sent a thrill of hope through Kendall. "Please," she whispered. "Can you help me get out of here?"

The woman opened her mouth to say something, but at that moment the room grew dark again as someone moved into the doorway. He was so large that every inch of sunlight was blocked.

The young woman quickly shook her head and put her fingertip to her lips.

When he stepped inside, the trapped sunlight spilled into the room behind him, backlighting him in a way that kept his face in shadows. Kendall had only a glimpse of his features, but that was enough. She knew where she was now, and the dread in her chest turned to bile in her throat. She wanted to scream, but it would be pointless because no one would hear her. No one would help her. She was now at Leo Kittering's mercy. Just the way he had planned it.

"Leave us!" he said to Maria.

She scurried out of the room without a backward glance.

Kendall sensed more than saw Kittering's smile. "It's been a long time."

She said nothing.

"Do you remember me?"

"Yes."

As he moved inside, Kendall saw him more clearly now. In the five years since they'd come face to face, he'd aged. He had to be well into his sixties, and the extra weight added even more years. His hair had gone completely gray, and he wore it combed back, highlighting the deep crevices in his forehead. The lower part of his face was hidden by a thick beard and mustache, also gray.

"You've changed," he said.

"So have you."

He smiled again. "The ravages of age, I'm afraid, but you..." He rested both hands on the silver head of his cane as he stood staring down at her. "The difference is remarkable. I'm not sure I would have recognized you." He cocked his head, studying her. "I've seen photos, of course, but it's still a shock. Graham Hollister...what does he think of the way you look?"

Kendall wanted to tell him that Graham would

love her no matter what, that nothing Kittering could do would tear them apart. But she knew that wasn't true. Graham was decent and caring, but no man could forgive what she'd done.

She looked down at her hands. Her once-manicured nails were chipped and dirty, and she thought them symbolic of her downfall. "Why are you doing this? Why couldn't you let us live in peace?"

Kittering's laugh was harsh. "The way you let my son live in peace? The question you should be asking is...why did I wait so long?"

"Why did you?"

"Timing is everything, as they say. Five years ago, I wanted you dead. Nothing would have pleased me more than finding your charred corpse in the wreckage at the bottom of that cliff. But...you survived somehow. You were a lot stronger than I gave you credit for and far more clever. You not only survived your injuries but you thrived." He shifted his weight, as if accommodating a painful leg or knee. "Oh, I could have ended it all, of course, at any time I wanted. Paid off a doctor to botch a surgery, a nurse to give you the wrong medication. Or I could have sent someone to your room to cut your throat while you slept. So very tempting," he said with a smile.

"But I soon came to see the merit of waiting until you made a full recovery, until everything in your life was perfect—the perfect husband, the perfect house, the perfect life...even a perfect new face—before I took everything from you. It hurts so much more that way, doesn't it? When you have so much to lose? That's what I call the perfect justice."

"This is not justice. This is nothing but revenge." Kendall was terrified, but she would not have him see her cower in fear. "After all the lives you've destroyed with your filthy business, don't you dare talk to me about justice."

"And after what you did to my son, don't you dare talk to me about vengeance." His gaze raked over her in the dim light. "I would have thought your current predicament would have curbed your tongue, but I can see that I was wrong. You may look like a different person, but underneath that plastic surface, you're still the same cold-hearted bitch who murdered my son."

"It was self defense. Deep down, you must know that."

"How convenient that you're the only one left alive to tell the story. But you're forgetting something. I knew my son. He was my heart and soul. When you killed him, you took everything from me."

Kendall tried to stay calm. She told herself she had to reason with him, try to reach him somehow and make him see her side of it. She hadn't murdered his son in cold blood. She'd defended herself from the cruel, selfish monster Leo Kittering had created. But he would never see it that way. He would never accept who his son really was.

"Nothing you do will bring him back." She was

ashamed of the tremor in her voice. She had faced Leo Kittering before and done so without an ounce of fear. But he was right. Things changed when you had so much to lose.

"Nothing will bring my son back, but watching you suffer will bring me a great deal of satisfaction," he said. "Your destruction is the only thing left for me to care about. It's the only thing I've lived for since L.J.'s death."

For a moment, Kendall merely stared at him. Then to her horror, her eyes filled with tears, and she did the one thing she'd always sworn never to do. Not even her stepfather's fist had moved her to beg for mercy, but she did so now without hesitation. "Please don't do anything to Graham. This isn't about him. It's me you want. Leave him out of this."

Kittering smiled. "It's too late. He's already in it. By the time I'm through with him, you won't even recognize him. The man you knew will be gone forever."

Kendall's blood turned to ice. "What are you going to do to him?"

"I won't need to lay a finger on him. He'll do it to himself. The things he'll do to get you back will destroy him."

"You don't know him," she said.

"You're wrong. I know exactly who I'm dealing with. And if by some miracle you both come out of this alive…it won't matter because the Graham Hollister you knew will be dead. And that'll be on your conscience because you're the one who brought him into this, not me."

He stood staring down at her for a moment longer, then turned and left the room. When the door closed behind him, Kendall was once again in darkness. She got up and rushed over to the door, but it was no use. Leo Kittering wouldn't make the mistake of leaving her cell unlocked. He had too many plans for her. And for Graham.

Kendall walked back over to the bed. She could lie down and close her eyes, make everything around her disappear. She knew how to do that. She'd learned a long time ago how to escape a cruel man's persecution.

Funny how all those tricks came back now in a time of distress.

But Leo Kittering wasn't her stepfather. He was a million times worse, and Kendall knew that he would never relent. He blamed her for his son's death, and now Graham would be made to suffer for her sins.

Unless she could find a way out.

Chapter Seven

Graham finally went to bed just after dawn, but an hour later he was back up. He showered and dressed and got ready for work, but he still wasn't convinced leaving the house was a good idea.

However, one of the things that Heller had cautioned him about the night before was the necessity of maintaining a normal routine. If Graham started acting strangely or deviated from his usual activities, people around him might start asking questions that could inadvertently put them in harm's way.

Graham's main concern in that regard was his assistant, Maggie Scofield. She'd called that morning as soon as she heard about the shooting. Graham hadn't been prepared to deal with her or anyone else so he'd let the call go to his voicemail.

But even if he stayed home, he wouldn't be able to put her off for long. Not Maggie. He'd always appreciated her loyalty and devotion to her job, but her doggedness could sometimes try his patience.

Nothing got past her, which made her an excellent assistant but not someone he could easily deceive.

She had an uncanny knack for reading his moods, even over the phone. One look at his face and she'd know something was wrong. The very last thing Graham needed was Maggie Scofield playing snoop.

He arrived at the office early—long before anyone else was around—so that he would have time to get settled before he had to face the staff. Hurrying into his office, he closed the door, sat down at his desk and turned on his computer.

Several projects in various stages of design and construction required his attention, but concentrating on anything other than the kidnapping was impossible. He didn't even go through the motions. Instead, he scoured the Internet for information on Gabriel Esteban and Leo Kittering.

He struck out with Esteban, which didn't surprise him. The man was undoubtedly using an alias. Graham had a little more luck with Leo Kittering. The name came up twice, both times in conjunction with articles about a racecar driver named L. J. Kittering, who had been killed five years earlier. But his death hadn't been the result of a racing accident as Graham had expected to find. He'd been murdered, but the details of the crime were sketchy.

Graham read the articles over and over, as if memorizing every word would somehow help him divine

Kendall's whereabouts. But it was no use. He'd gleaned very little information, and he didn't know how to apply it to what he already knew.

Swiveling in his chair, he stared out the window, a pulse throbbing in his temple. The air was cool in his office, but he suddenly felt clammy with sweat as he tried to make sense of what he'd read.

He thought again about his separation from Kendall, her move to Mexico and the car accident that had nearly taken her life. And as he absently watched the vapor trail of a jet etch the clear sky, he let himself think about the unthinkable.

Had Kendall been involved in L. J. Kittering's death?

She'd been living in Mexico at the time. According to the FBI, she'd even worked for Kittering's father, Leo. So she definitely had a connection to the family, but it was a stretch to think she might have had something to do with the son's murder. Heller said that Leo Kittering operated one of the largest drug cartels in Mexico. It would be far less of a stretch to assume L.J. had been taken out by a rival drug lord.

But, of course, that was nothing but speculation. The result of Graham's imagination going a little crazy because he didn't know what the hell was going on.

Absently he massaged the taut muscles at the back of his neck as he tried to remember everything Heller had told him about Leo Kittering.

He was an American who had fled across the border after being charged with serious crimes, including extortion. Over the years, he'd built a drug empire in Mexico and was now virtually untouchable.

But that was something else Graham didn't understand. If the FBI had known where he was all this time, why hadn't they had him extradited? Was he so powerful that even the United States government couldn't touch him?

That a man like Kittering could be behind Kendall's kidnapping was inconceivable to Graham. How was it that his nice, safe world had suddenly collided with that of a notorious drug lord?

The whole situation still seemed like a bad dream. The shooting, the kidnapping, the home invasion by Gabriel Esteban and his band of thugs. Even the involvement of the FBI. The *FBI* for God's sake.

Graham's only previous run-ins with the law had been speeding and parking tickets, and now, suddenly, his incoming calls were being monitored, his house had been swept for listening devices and he'd been interrogated by a federal agent who seemed to have an agenda other than tracking Kendall's kidnappers.

Twenty-four hours ago, his biggest worry had been getting everything wrapped up at the office before he and Kendall left on vacation. Now he didn't know if he would ever see her again.

He scrubbed a hand across his face. His helplessness

left him restless, angry and afraid. How the hell had any of this happened? How had his life spiraled so completely out of control in the space of only one day?

Graham still had a hard time accepting the fact that he couldn't pick up the phone and hear Kendall's voice. He couldn't believe that his own family was being watched at that very moment, their lives in danger unless he did exactly as Esteban ordered.

And just who was Gabriel Esteban? Had Kittering hired him to do his dirty work?

Esteban hadn't struck him as the type who would follow another man's orders. There was too much macho pride in his eyes, his smile, the way he held himself. Esteban wasn't the subservient type. So what was *his* connection to Leo Kittering?

"Graham?"

Startled, Graham whirled to find Maggie standing on the other side of his desk, staring down at him with a puzzled frown. He had no idea how long she'd been there. He'd been so deep in thought he hadn't heard the door open.

"What's up?" The casual greeting sounded strained and unnatural. The inflection didn't go unnoticed by Maggie, whose scowl deepened as she continued to study him.

As always, she was dressed impeccably in a dark suit and starched blouse, even though Graham's firm was much less formal than her previous employer. But Maggie was old-school and particular about her professional wardrobe. She would never dream of showing up at work in jeans or even khakis. Her nails were always done, her dark hair pulled back out of the way and today a pencil was tucked neatly behind one ear.

She cocked her head. "You okay?"

Graham carefully schooled his expression before he answered. "Sure," he said with a shrug. "Why do you ask?"

"For one thing, you've been holed up in here all morning. That's not like you. You're usually going stir-crazy long before now. For another..." She paused. "You look like hell."

"Long night," Graham muttered. "I didn't sleep well."

"When did you get back? I thought you and Kendall were spending the night in Houston."

"We decided to come back last night."

"Well, that explains why I didn't get an answer at the hotel this morning. I also called your cell phone. You didn't get my message?"

"No, sorry. Was it something important?"

Absently she straightened a stack of papers on the corner of his desk. "I just wanted to touch base after I heard about the assassination attempt on the news this morning. They said the ambassador was the only one hurt, but I couldn't help worrying because I knew you were all there last night. Everyone's okay, right?"

Graham glanced away. "Yeah, everyone's fine."

"Were you there when it happened?"

"Yes, but I didn't see anything," he said quickly, hoping to head her off.

But no such luck. Maggie was just getting warmed up.

"They said on the news that the police don't even have a suspect in custody, which means the shooter is still at large. No telling where he is by now." She kept fiddling with the papers on his desk. "How in the world does someone walk into a crowded room with a gun and shoot an ambassador, of all people? Didn't he have bodyguards? And why haven't any witnesses come forward? Someone must have seen something."

"I don't know," Graham said. "All I can tell you is that there were a lot of people at that reception. And no one expected to see something like that."

"Yes, I'm sure that's true. Some of the talking heads are saying it could be a conspiracy. Someone in the ambassador's inner circle could have been in on the plan. Or someone hired by the private firm that supplied security could have been bought off. They think at the very least that the gunman had help getting in and out of the building."

"No one knows that for sure. We'll just have to wait and see what the investigation turns up."

Maggie nodded. "Graham, do you think the shooting had something to do with the ambassador's connection to PemCo Oil? There's been trouble brewing ever since they made that deal with Pemex."

"You're asking the wrong person. I'm just an architect. World politics is a little out of my league."

"But don't you think—"

"Maggie, for God's sake, give it a rest!" he blurted in frustration. "I already said I don't know anything about it."

Her gray eyes mirrored her shock at his outburst. He rarely raised his voice and never to her. "Sure, fine. I was just curious, that's all."

"I know you are, but I'm not in the mood to speculate endlessly about what happened. Let's just let the authorities sort it out." He paused, drew a deep breath and tried to muster up a half smile. "Sorry I snapped. Short fuse this morning."

She shrugged, but her gaze was still curious. More so now than before.

"No harm done. You're entitled to blow every once in a while. Let's us know you're human."

Oh, I'm human, all right. "I appreciate that. Was there something else you wanted?"

"Yes, as a matter of fact. I came in to tell you that Michael Barron called a few minutes ago. He's on his way up."

"He's in Austin? Why?"

"He didn't say, just that he needs to talk to you and I'm not to let you leave until he arrives. What should I tell him when he gets here?"

"Yes, Graham. What do you want her to tell me?" Michael echoed as he breezed into the office.

Maggie lifted a brow at the sudden tension in the room, but Graham merely shrugged.

"Would either of you like some coffee?" she said. "I was just heading downstairs to get some."

"Not for me," Michael said. "But thanks anyway."

"Graham?"

"No, thanks." He watched warily as Michael took the seat across from his desk. "What are you doing here?"

"Come on, Graham. You know why I'm here. You missed your appointment with Terrence. You were supposed to come by the office and sign the contracts this morning. Or did you forget?"

"There was a change in plans. I came back to Austin last night."

"I heard. I thought you might be a little distracted this morning so I decided to bring the contracts to you."

Graham frowned. "Why would you think I'd be distracted?"

"After what happened? I imagine we're all a little rattled." Michael set his briefcase on the edge of Graham's desk and flipped open the latches. "I don't know about you, but it's not every day I attend a party where someone gets shot. Much less an ambassador."

So they were back to that. The assassination attempt was all anyone wanted to talk about. Graham supposed he should be grateful that the focus wasn't on him. "Maggie says it's all over the news."

"You mean you haven't turned on the TV?"

Michael glanced up in surprise. "The feds are all over this thing. They're interviewing everyone who was there last night, including the wait staff, security, you name it. They already talk to you?"

"Briefly."

Michael nodded. "CNN had someone on this morning who used to work for the Department of Homeland Security. He thinks it may have been a terrorist attack. This is a big deal, Graham. I'm surprised you don't seem more interested."

"Just because I'm not talking about it incessantly doesn't mean I'm not interested. Some of us have work to do."

"Or maybe you've got something else on your mind." Michael took out the contracts and slid them across the desk.

"What's that supposed to mean?"

"I'm talking about you and Kendall. Something happened last night, didn't it?"

Graham picked up a pen and toyed with the top for a moment before he realized the nervous tic gave away his agitation. Carefully, he laid the pen aside. "Kendall and I are fine."

"Then why is she missing?"

Graham froze. "Who told you that?"

"Terrence said you talked to Ellie last night, and you were worried because Kendall left the reception without saying anything. Then she called and wanted to meet you at home, but when you drove back, she wasn't there. Something is going on, Graham. Why don't you just save us both a lot of trouble and tell me what it is because I'm not going back to Houston until you do."

Graham gave him a warning look. "This is none of your business. Just leave it alone."

"Then something *is* wrong?"

"I didn't say that."

"Damn it, Graham." Michael ran a hand through his hair in frustration. "Enough with the stoicism, okay? How the hell am I supposed to help you if you won't level with me?"

"Did I ask for your help?"

Michael sat back with a heavy sigh. "I knew it. Kendall's left you again, hasn't she? That's why she didn't want you to know about the money."

A muscle in Graham's leg began to twitch. He needed to get up and pace, but he made himself sit completely still. "What money?"

"The hundred thousand she wanted to borrow. Ellie told Terrence and me everything." At Graham's look, Michael said quickly, "Now, don't be mad at her. She's worried sick about you."

"I'm not mad. But there's no need for any of you to worry. As you can see, I'm perfectly fine." But by this time the muscle in his leg was like a jackhammer. "I'll sign the contracts and you can hand-deliver them to Terrence yourself."

"What about Kendall?"

"What about her?"

Michael's gaze bored into his. "You don't know where she is, do you?"

Graham glanced down at the contracts. "It's not what you think. Kendall and I are going to be fine. We just need to be left alone to work this out on our own."

"Work what out?"

"I'm not going to talk about this with you."

"Fine, if that's the way you want it."

"It is."

Michael lifted his hands in resignation. "All right. I won't say anything more about it. Just know this, though. If you need to talk or if you need my help with anything, I'm only a phone call away."

Graham nodded, his chest heavy with the need to talk. But he didn't dare. "I appreciate that."

"One other thing…"

"Yeah?"

Michael's expression darkened as he leaned forward. "Do you have any idea why the FBI would be coming around asking questions about Kendall?"

Graham couldn't speak for a moment. His breath was suddenly shallow and rapid, and he felt light-headed. "When did this happen?"

"Earlier this morning. Two agents were in Terrence's office when I got to work. They were asking a lot of questions that didn't have anything to do with the shooting. What are they after, Graham?"

Graham tried to stay calm, but worry and stress

were taking a toll. And now to find out that the FBI was asking questions behind his back. What the hell were they up to?

"Graham?"

His gaze shot up. Michael was watching him intently. "I have no idea," he said truthfully. "It was probably just a routine follow-up after the shooting. Like you said, they're interviewing everyone who was at the reception last night."

Michael shrugged. "Yeah, maybe. But hypothetically speaking, if you *were* in some kind of trouble, you know you could come to me, right? I'd do everything I could to help you."

Emotion welled in Graham's throat. He wanted to tell Michael everything. He needed desperately to talk to someone he trusted. But the more people he brought into this, the greater the risk.

"I know you would," he said. "And if I were in trouble, you'd be the first one I'd call."

"I hope you mean that. I don't know what the hell is going on and it's obvious that you don't want to tell me. But be careful, Graham. I've seen this sort of thing before when I worked for the D.A. If I didn't know better, I'd say the feds are trying to nail you with something. Make damn sure you don't fall into any of their traps."

Traps? Graham's mind worked frantically. The agents were the good guys, weren't they? They were supposed to be on his side. He had to believe that.

"Thanks for the warning, but I'm not the target of their investigation. There's nothing to worry about."

"That's the thing, though," Michael said slowly. "You don't always know you're the target until it's too late."

A chill slid up Graham's spine as Heller's questions about Kendall came back to him. And now agents were interrogating his family. They wouldn't do that if Graham wasn't considered a suspect. But what crime did they think he'd committed? Surely to God they didn't think he'd kidnapped his own wife.

"Look, if you don't want to talk to me, then let me recommend an attorney," Michael said worriedly. "Even if the questions are routine, what would be the harm in bringing someone in who is looking out for your best interests?"

"I appreciate the offer, but I don't need an attorney."

"With all due respect, I think you do," Michael said. "You'd better wise up before it's too late."

Their eyes locked for the longest moment, and then Graham dropped his gaze, pretending to read over the contracts while he bought himself some time.

Was Michael right? Was the FBI setting a trap for him while they only pretended to help him find Kendall?

Graham thought again of his conversation with Heller. He'd sensed the agent was after something right from the start. The meeting had been more like an interrogation than an interview, and Graham supposed that part of it *was* routine. In criminal investigations, family members, particularly spouses, were always the first to be scrutinized.

Surely he should have been cleared by now, though. There was nothing in his background that would arouse suspicion.

But for some reason, the FBI still had questions about his relationship with Kendall, and Graham didn't have a good feeling about the outcome of their investigation. Because if they didn't believe him, how were they going to help him get his wife back?

He picked up a pen to sign the contracts, then realized how badly his hands were shaking. He glanced up. Michael had seen and now his gaze narrowed. Graham could tell that he was on the verge of saying something else, but he shook his head slightly, warning him off. Michael frowned but kept silent.

Graham scrawled his name in the designated places, then restacked the contracts. Before he handed them back to Michael, he stuck a Post-it note to the top and scribbled a message: Can't talk here. Meet me downstairs. Coffee shop.

He shoved the documents across the desk and watched as Michael took them. He skimmed the note, glanced up with another question in his eyes, but Graham shook his head again.

Michael very deliberately opened his briefcase and tucked the contracts inside. He closed the latches and stood. "That should do it. I'm sure Terrence will be relieved to have this matter taken care of."

"Sorry you had to drive all the way up here," Graham said.

"No problem. It was a nice drive and I always like an excuse to get out of the office." Michael glanced at his watch. "Look, I hate leaving things on a tense note. I'm sorry if I came on too strong. The lawyer in me gets a little carried away at times."

"I know, but everything's fine."

"If you say so."

"Tell Terrence if he has any questions, he can call me."

"Will do."

A FEW MINUTES later, Graham walked down to the coffee shop on the lower level. Michael had snagged a table in the corner, instinctively leaving the chair facing the door for Graham so that he could watch the traffic in and out of the shop.

"What's going on?" he said anxiously when Graham sat down across from him. "What's with the clandestine note?"

Graham tried to study their surroundings casually. He wondered if they were being watched. By Esteban's men? By the FBI? He was starting to worry about who his real enemy was.

"I need to tell you something," he finally said. "But you can't react. You can't let it show on your face. Anyone glancing over here has to be convinced that we're not discussing anything more serious than the Astros' playoff chances."

"Hey, that *is* serious," Michael said with a grin, then when he saw Graham's face, he sobered. "Go on. I'm listening." To his credit, his expression remained neutral as he picked up his coffee and took a sip.

As quickly as he could, Graham told him everything, starting with Kendall leaving the reception, her phone call, Esteban's ultimatum and the FBI's interest in the time Kendall had spent in Mexico before her accident.

When he was finished, Michael took a long moment to respond. He kept his eyes on his cup, but when he spoke, his voice was hushed with shock. "My God. This is unbelievable."

"I know it is. I still have a hard time believing it's not just a bad dream. I keep thinking I'll wake up and everything will be exactly as it was before Kendall and I went to that reception. If anything happens to her or to anyone in my family...I'm not sure how I'd handle it."

"You must be going crazy."

Graham gave a little smile. "That's putting it mildly. And now after what you said about the FBI questioning Terrence, I'm starting to wonder if I did the right thing calling them in. If they think I'm guilty of something, how hard will they look for Kendall's kidnappers?"

"Yeah, that worries me, too," Michael said. "But for what's it worth, I'd have done the same thing. Your wife goes missing, you call the cops to help find her. She gets kidnapped, you call in the FBI. You want to believe they're on your side. But I meant what I said earlier. Be careful with these guys."

"What do you think they're after?"

"I don't know. I've still got some friends in the Harris County D.A.'s office. I'll ask around, see if anyone's heard anything."

"What should I do in the meantime?"

"The one thing you don't do is answer any more questions. Keep your mouth shut until we get you a lawyer."

"Isn't that going to make me look guilty of something?"

Michael's gaze lifted. "As of now, we're more interested in protecting your rights than we are in appearances."

Graham tried to swallow past the fear in his throat. "You think it's that serious?"

"Put it this way. Your wife has been kidnapped, your home broken into, your family threatened. And what do the feds focus on? *You.* So, yeah, I'd say it's that serious."

"How the hell does something like this happen to someone like me? I'm not mixed up with criminals. I don't live that kind of life."

"Well, now you do," Michael said grimly.

"Someone's doing a real number on you, buddy. The feds, this guy Esteban." He shook his head. "No wonder you're going out of your mind."

Graham had no idea why Michael's sympathy meant so much to him, but it felt good to talk to someone he completely trusted. Someone who had no hidden agendas. "I'm glad I told you."

"So am I. And don't worry, okay? I'm going to see you through this. As soon as I leave here, I'll start making some calls. You'll have the best defense attorney in the state within the hour."

"Thanks."

"In the meantime, tell me again about the interview with Heller."

Graham went through it a second time. When he finished, he said wearily, "Have you ever heard of this man Kittering?"

"I've heard of the son, L.J. I even met him a few years back. He approached Hollister Motors about customizing one of our engines for his race cars. He had a whole fleet of them as I recall."

"What happened?"

"The deal fell through. I was never clear on all the details, but I think Terrence was under the impression that Kittering was not someone he wanted to do business with."

"Meaning?"

Michael toyed with his coffee cup. "I guess you may as well know. Kendall started seeing L.J. while he was in Houston. They met through Terrence, of all people, and I know he felt pretty rotten about it. You were in L.A. at the time," he hurriedly added. "You and Kendall were headed for a divorce so it wasn't exactly like she betrayed you. But Terrence still felt bad for bringing them together."

Graham was surprised by the jolt of anger that shot through him. He hadn't exactly been a Boy Scout during their separation, so he shouldn't have expected that Kendall would behave any differently. But he didn't want to think about her being with another man even if the relationship had occurred years ago while they were apart.

"How did it end?"

Michael sighed. "It didn't. When Kittering went back to Mexico, Kendall followed him."

Graham's hands tightened into fists. He turned away so that Michael couldn't see his eyes. "So that's how she ended up in Mexico."

Kendall's involvement with Kittering explained a lot. No wonder she'd been so reluctant to renew their vows. She'd still had feelings for another man.

"She got a job and an apartment down there," Michael said. "I don't think she planned on ever coming back. And then she had the accident."

"Was she still with Kittering then?"

"I honestly don't know. I tried to call her a few times after she first got down there, just to make sure everything was okay. She wouldn't tell me anything, but I sensed that things weren't working out the way she'd hoped. That's when I called and told you about her move. I thought someone should know just in case she ran into trouble."

"What kind of trouble?"

Michael shrugged. "She was alone in a foreign country. Anything could have happened."

"Did you know that Kittering was murdered?"

Michael's mouth thinned. "Yeah, I read something about it."

"Was Kendall involved?"

"What?" Michael looked genuinely shocked. "Why on earth would you think that?"

"The timing, for one thing. She followed him to Mexico and then he turned up dead. And now this. Kidnappings in this country are rare, Michael. Especially kidnappings for ransom. I keep asking myself how Kendall and I ended up as targets."

"You've got money, connections. Maybe it's as simple as that."

"What about the FBI? Why are they asking questions about our relationship? Why are they trying to dig up dirt on our marriage when they should be looking for Kendall?"

"The assassination attempt is their top priority right now. They're probably feeling heat all the way from the White House. They'll need to find something pretty damn fast in order to cover their own asses."

The muscle was hammering in Graham's leg

again, and his head felt ready to explode. He needed to sleep, but he suddenly wanted a drink more. "Why the hell would they think I had anything to do with the shooting? That's crazy."

"Is it? Think about it, Graham. Your wife used to live in Mexico. Who knows what kind of people she got involved with down there?"

Graham just stared at him. "You're not serious."

"I'm just thinking about how the feds may be looking at this. They'll exploit every connection they can find, no matter how obscure."

"You're scaring the hell out of me, Michael."

"I don't mean to. It's entirely possible I'm reading the situation all wrong," he said, but his demeanor belied his optimism. "At any rate, I'll feel a whole lot better when we have an attorney on board."

Chapter Eight

At two o'clock that afternoon, Graham heard from the kidnappers. He'd placed the phone on the desk beside his computer, and for a moment after it rang, he just stared at it. Then he lifted it to his ear.

"Hollister."

"The first installment is two million dollars. A piece of cake for a guy like you. You have twenty-four hours."

The voice was electronically altered, but for some reason, Graham didn't think the caller was Gabriel Esteban. He couldn't distinguish an accent, and the speech pattern and word choices were much less formal. "That's not enough time."

"Twenty-four hours," the caller reiterated. "No cops, no FBI, no surveillance. You come alone."

"Where?"

"We'll be in touch."

The call ended and Graham slowly lowered the phone to his desk. He didn't know whether to be relieved or terrified that something was finally happening.

AFTER CONTACTING Heller, Graham spent the rest of the afternoon on the phone with his stockbroker and bank. By five o'clock, he'd arranged to pick up the money the following morning, and now all that was left to do was wait some more.

He stopped by a barbecue place on his way home from work and picked up enough dinner for two. Agent Jones seemed to appreciate the effort, and they ate in silence at the kitchen table while Myron wolfed down his dinner nearby.

Graham thought about asking the agent why the FBI had gone to see his brother, but then he remembered Michael's warning to say nothing without an attorney. He decided to keep his questions to himself so that he didn't inadvertently trigger more suspicion.

Afterward, he went outside for a walk. He let Myron out, too, and the cat shot off in the dark. Graham would have liked the company, but the feline obviously had other things on his mind.

Graham strode down to the summerhouse and sat on the steps for a long time, listening to the water rush over the rocks and to the crickets that were beginning to sing from the woods.

Twilight fell and he still didn't move. He thought about everything Michael had told him that morning. Kendall had fallen for a race-car driver named L. J. Kittering. Graham couldn't imagine a profession that contrasted more starkly with his. He tried to picture what Kittering might have been like, but the images storming through his head made him ill.

He reminded himself that he and Kendall had been separated at the time. They were headed for a divorce. Graham had seen other people while they were apart. What did it matter that Kendall had, too?

But who he was he kidding? There was a stark difference in the casual dates he'd had and Kendall's relationship with Kittering. She'd followed him back to Mexico. She'd started a whole new life for herself with another man in a foreign country. There was nothing casual about that.

According to Michael, she hadn't planned on ever coming back. And then Kittering was murdered and she'd been in a terrible car accident.

Had she still been in love with Kittering when Graham had come to the hospital to see her? Had she been mourning him all through her own painful recovery?

Graham knew it did no good to dwell on the past, but he couldn't help it tonight. He couldn't help wondering about a lot of things in Kendall's life.

But nothing he'd learned changed the way he felt about her. He still loved her. He would still do everything in his power to bring her home safely.

The mosquitoes came out as the twilight deepened, and he finally went back to the house. He tried to watch TV for a while, but it was no use. He couldn't concentrate on anything now but the impending drop.

What if something went wrong? What if Esteban knew he had brought in the FBI? What if he somehow mixed up the directions and went to the wrong location?

A million things could go wrong, and Graham's family would pay the price if he screwed this up.

He tried to be encouraged by Delacourt's assurance that the feds knew what they were doing. But it wasn't so easy to trust them now that Graham knew he had become a person of interest in their investigation.

Two days ago, such a thing would have been unthinkable. But someone had taken control of Graham's life, and now he was learning very quickly that he had to watch his back.

He lay on top of the bed and stared at the ceiling. The lights were off, but he hadn't closed the shutters and moonlight flooded in.

He'd had only an hour or so of sleep in the last twenty-four hours, and he had to be fresh and rested for the drop. But he couldn't shut off his thoughts. He couldn't stop thinking about the what-ifs, both past and present.

Rolling over, he stared at Kendall's picture on the nightstand. Her face was at once familiar and strange, her smile both tentative and alluring. She'd always been a complicated woman, always had her secrets. Maybe that was why Graham had been so fascinated by her. She was different from him. He'd always known what he wanted and had planned his life accordingly. Kendall had lived in the moment.

But the accident had changed that, too. The injuries had not only eroded her strength and vitality, but her confidence and zest. She'd seemed so unsure of herself when she first came home from the hospital, and that wasn't like the woman he'd married.

Graham thought back to the night he'd first brought her to this house. She'd come out of the bathroom smelling of the jasmine that grew in the garden, her skin warm and silky-smooth from her bath.

She'd slipped into bed, drawing the covers up to her chin. When he reached for her, she pulled away, closing her eyes as she said on a ragged whisper, "How can you want me? I'm nothing but skin and bones, and I have all these scars."

She had lost a lot of weight after the accident. She was much too thin and her eyes seemed filled with a wariness Graham hadn't remembered from before. But none of that mattered to him.

He took her hand and guided her to him. "Does that feel like I don't want you?"

She shivered. "I want you, too, Graham. But what if I disappoint you? It's been so long since we were together."

He smiled. "It'll be okay."

She turned, her gaze searching his face in the dark. "I need to tell you about Mexico."

"Now?" He gave her pained look. "Are you sure

it can't wait?" He drew her even closer, feeling her tremble against him.

"If I don't tell you now…"

"Whatever it is, it doesn't matter. We've both made a lot of mistakes, Kendall. But this is a new start. Whatever happened in the past should stay there."

"Do you mean that?"

"Yes, I do. I think it's the only way we can make this work. No looking back, no regrets." He stroked her back. "And anyway, I think we've done enough talking for one night."

He held her for a long time until she finally began to relax. Then she lifted her face to his for a kiss.

The first time they came together had been fast. Graham hadn't wanted it to be that way. Kendall still seemed so fragile to him.

But her hands had been too eager, too daring, and when she trailed her lips over his chest, skimmed her tongue down his stomach, when her hand lowered to tease and caress, he couldn't hold back.

The urgency with which they made love had shocked and thrilled him. Kendall had always been a passionate woman, but that night she seemed almost frantic to have him.

The second time had been slower, more languid, and afterward, when he held her again, he could sense that something had changed. Her earlier doubts had slipped away. For the first time since he'd seen her in the hospital, she seemed to have regained some of her confidence. For a moment at least, he'd glimpsed a bit of the old Kendall. A woman he had neither the will nor the desire to resist. A woman he would gladly kill for if it came to that.

Turning, he stared at her side of the bed, feeling more lonely and scared than he'd ever been his life. Because, as vivid as his memories were, the images of his wife with another man were starting to crowd them out.

KENDALL DREAMED about Graham that night. They were on a beach somewhere, lying close, their bodies warm from the sun.

She rolled over and stared up at the sky. The day was so beautiful, and yet as she watched, black clouds moved toward them over the water. The storm came inland at a terrifying speed.

She sat up in alarm. "Graham, we can't stay here. We have to get some place safe."

"There is no safe place, Kendall."

She turned. Suddenly the man beside her wasn't Graham, but L. J. Kittering. He looked exactly the way she remembered him. Dark, handsome and utterly charming…until she looked into his eyes.

Kendall tried to turn from those eyes now, but they were too hypnotic. She couldn't tear her gaze away. "What do you want?"

"The same thing my father wants. Justice."

"Where's Graham?" she screamed. "What have you done to him?"

He smiled. "Exactly what you did to me."

He turned slowly and Kendall followed his gaze to the water. The storm clouds were almost overhead now and the landscape darkened. In a flash of lightning, she saw Graham lying on the beach, a knife blade protruding from his chest as blood gushed from the wound.

She started to run to him but someone held her back. All she could do was watch helplessly as water cascaded over his body, washing away the blood as the tide carried him out to sea where he would be lost to her forever.

She tried to tear free from her captor, but he held her fast, turning her so that she had to look up into his face. It was Michael Barron. His smile was exactly like L. J. Kittering's. Why had she never noticed how much alike they were?

"It's too late. Your little game is over. You played us all, but now you've lost everything. Graham is gone. He's never coming back."

He started to laugh then, and she saw L.J. standing behind him. He was laughing, too. They were all laughing. Leo Kittering. Terrence and Ellie. Even Maggie Scofield…

Kendall's gasp woke her up. Her heart pounded, and her skin was damp and clammy. She gazed around, remembering where she was, and panic exploded in her chest.

"What have I done?" she whispered into the darkness.

Chapter Nine

At two o'clock the next afternoon—exactly twenty-four hours after the first contact—the second call came in. Graham had the money ready, and he'd been briefed by Special Agent Heller on what to expect and how to respond to various scenarios.

He didn't wear a wire. They'd agreed that it would be too risky, but he could still be tracked using the GPS chip in his personal cell phone. If he was searched, the phone would be tossed, but at least its presence wouldn't necessarily arouse suspicion.

The caller had instructed Graham to place the money in a briefcase, take the elevator downstairs and walk out the front entrance of the building without a word to anyone. Maggie had tried to waylay him when he came out of his office, but Graham had mumbled something about being late for an appointment and hurried past her desk without stopping.

The sun was glaring outside. He put on his sunglasses as he started walking down the street. His office was located downtown and pedestrian traffic was heavy. He found himself studying the faces of the people he met.

The man carrying a briefcase similar to Graham's…was he one of the kidnappers?

The brunette in the mini skirt…was she there to pick up the money?

Esteban's phone rang and Graham quickly lifted it to his ear. "Yes?"

"Head north toward the Capitol. There's a phone booth five blocks from where you are now. The phone will ring in exactly five minutes."

Graham's head shot up as he once again searched his surroundings. Was he being watched? Or was he being traced by the GPS chip in the phone Esteban had given him?

It hit him suddenly how privacy had been eroded by modern technology. He'd never really thought about it before, but now he felt almost claustrophobic as he walked down the street.

The traffic lights took longer than he anticipated, and after the third block, he began to worry about the time. Sweat trickled down his back as he picked up his pace. He was almost jogging by the time he reached the phone kiosk. Then he worried whether or not he was at the right one. He hadn't been given an address.

Turning, he spotted another kiosk across the street. *Damn.* Which one?

Clutching the briefcase, he waited.

After a few moments, he started to panic. Should he cross the street, check out the other phone?

He glanced at his watch. The five minutes since the last call had long since come and gone, and the pay phone remained silent. Something had gone wrong.

The tightness in his chest intensified. Graham had almost decided to cross to the other side of the street when the pay phone finally rang. He spun and grabbed for it, oblivious of the curious gazes from some of the passersby.

"There's a cell phone taped to the bottom of the stand. Turn it on and throw the other one away," the altered voice instructed.

Graham felt underneath the kiosk and located the phone. Placing his body so that no one on the street could observe him, he ripped off the duct tape and removed it. He turned on the phone, waited for it to power up, then threw the unit Esteban had given him into a nearby trash can.

And then he waited again.

As he stood on the street anticipating the next call, Graham thought about his latest instructions. The scenario was playing out like a clichéd movie scene. The altered voice, the hidden cell phone. It was almost as if Esteban was mocking him, and Graham wondered suddenly if the whole thing was a trap.

He tried to keep his cool, but he was getting more nervous by the moment. The day was warm, but the sweat beading on his forehead was more from stress than the heat.

When the phone finally rang, he stepped back into the shade of a building to answer, his gaze automatically scanning the area. "Yes?"

"Are you familiar with the Orchid Tree Restaurant?"

The voice was unaltered this time and sounded American, but Graham still didn't recognize it.

"I know where it is." The restaurant was several blocks over from where he stood. The South-American cuisine was popular with the downtown lunch crowd, and Graham had eaten there on several occasions with clients.

"Ask to be seated on the terrace. Get a table near the street."

"What then?"

"Order a drink and wait."

The call ended and Graham started walking. By the time he got to the restaurant, it was close to two-thirty, and the lunch crowd had dispersed. He was able to get a table near the street without a problem, and as he pulled out the chair, he once again took stock of his surroundings.

A few tables over, four well-dressed women in their thirties laughed over a pitcher of margaritas. A couple sat holding hands at a corner table, and a young family—mother, father, two kids—came in for a late lunch. Dressed casually in jeans and T-shirts, they looked as if they'd spent the day at the park. The kids clutched balloons in their fists and after they were seated, the mother tied the ribbons to the backs of their chairs.

The balloons—one red, one yellow—bobbed like cork floaters in the breeze, and Graham stared for a long moment, not so much mesmerized by the movement, but by the family's happy faces.

He envied them their carefree smiles and he envied the couple in the corner, the friends laughing over drinks. He wanted to be having a quiet lunch with Kendall, discussing nothing more pressing than their plans for the rest of the afternoon instead of waiting for a call from her kidnappers.

The waitress seated another customer, a man who had come in alone. He wore khakis, a lightweight jacket and loafers without socks. He asked for two menus and ordered two drinks, as if expecting someone to join him. Despite the guy's understated demeanor, Graham was immediately suspicious, and he watched from the corner of his eye as he waited for the waitress to bring out his own drink.

One of the little boys inadvertently loosened the ribbon on the back of his chair, and the yellow balloon drifted up from the table. The father tried to grab it, but the breeze whipped the ribbon out of his reach and the balloon soared over the wrought-iron fence toward the street.

Rather than being distraught by the loss, the little boy squealed and clapped his hands, enthralled by the sight of the balloon as it drifted across the street, already high above the cars and still climbing as a draft pulled it skyward.

Graham watched it, too, the bright yellow vibrant against the blue sky. He was staring upward, his gaze still on the balloon, or he never would have seen it. A flash of light from the top of a nearby building.

A split second later, a loud *bang* on the patio caused him to half rise from his chair, his heart pounding against the wall of his chest.

For a split second, everything seemed to go deadly silent in the aftermath, and then embarrassed laughter erupted from the table of women as they glanced his way.

He realized then what had happened. The red balloon, still tied to the back of the second boy's chair, had popped and Graham had thought it was gunfire.

His gaze went back to the top of the building. Whatever he'd seen a moment ago was gone.

The phone he'd placed on the table vibrated and he quickly picked it up.

"Hello?"

"Do exactly as you're told or the next target won't be a balloon."

Graham's blood froze. Someone had fired at the patio. The bullet had gone through a balloon that floated mere inches from a child's head.

His hand started to shake.

"Are you listening, Mr. Hollister?"

He tightened his grip on the phone. "Yes."

"Take the money and leave the restaurant. Head back toward your office." It was the same voice he'd heard earlier, but the signal was clear this time, as if the caller was just around the corner.

Graham dropped some bills on the table, picked up the briefcase and rushed from the patio, anxious to put as much distance between himself and those kids as he could. As he crossed the street, the phone rang again.

"Mr. Hollister?"

A different voice this time, and Graham immediately recognized the accent. It was Esteban. "Yes?"

"The man who came into the restaurant after you. Did you notice him? He came in alone and ordered two drinks."

"I saw him," Graham said.

"He's a federal agent. When the balloon popped, he went for his gun."

Graham stopped in his tracks and a pedestrian behind him bumped into his shoulder. Graham murmured an apology as he moved toward the edge of the sidewalk. "I'm sure you're mistaken."

"No, Mr. Hollister, you are the one who has made a very terrible mistake. You broke the first rule. You brought in the FBI, and now someone close to you will die."

"No, don't…please. I have the money. It's yours. I'll do anything you ask just…don't hurt my family."

"You gambled and you lost. Perhaps next time you will think twice before you cross me."

The call ended abruptly, and Graham felt the sidewalk tilt beneath him. He couldn't think for a moment, he couldn't react. His heart was beating so hard he could hear the echo of it in his ears.

Someone close to him was about to die. How was he going to stop it?

He got out his personal cell phone and dialed the number Heller had given him. "You told me he wouldn't see your men," Graham all but shouted at the agent. "You assured me your people know what they're doing."

"Slow down a minute. What are you talking about?"

"Esteban spotted your man."

"What man?"

"On the terrace of the restaurant. Esteban had someone shoot a kid's balloon, and this guy went for his gun."

"Graham, calm down and listen. He wasn't one of ours. I don't know who he is, but he's not FBI."

Graham frowned. "You're sure?"

"Yes, of course, I'm sure. Esteban was bluffing."

"No, he wasn't. He knows you guys are involved, and now he's going after my family. We have to do something. If he gets near them—"

"All right, hang on," Heller said. "I'm sending a car. Stay where you are."

Two minutes later, a dark-colored Buick pulled to

the curb. Graham walked over and opened the door. He recognized the man behind the wheel. It was Andy Pinson, the agent who had helped sweep his house for bugs.

"Get in," the agent said.

Graham climbed in and slammed the door. "I need to see Heller."

"No problem. He wants to see you, too."

"Why?"

"He'll explain everything when he sees you." He pulled away from the curb into traffic.

"What about my family?"

"Heller is checking in with the surveillance teams now. Try not to worry. We've handled situations like this before. We know what we're doing."

He'd heard that line before, Graham thought grimly. And look where it had gotten him.

AT COUNTY Memorial Hospital in Lufkin, Texas, Audrey Hollister sat in her mother's hospital room reading the latest Mary Higgins Clark mystery. Usually, she had no problem losing herself in the story, but today she was so exhausted the text kept running together. Finally she laid the book aside and closed her eyes for a moment.

The surgery to repair her mother's hip had gone well, but now, two days later, the older woman was still in a lot of pain. She hadn't slept much the night before, nor had Audrey, and she was starting to feel the wear and tear of too many sedentary hours at her mother's bedside and too many cups of bad coffee. She wasn't so young herself anymore.

She needed to get something to eat, or at least take a brief walk. Anything to get out of that hospital room for a few minutes, but she didn't want to leave until the doctor had made his afternoon rounds. In spite of the successful surgery, her mother wasn't doing as well as Audrey had hoped, and she wanted some reassurance that the prognosis was still favorable.

The door to the hallway opened, and she jumped slightly, realizing that she'd dozed off for a moment. A woman in green scrubs walked in and gave her a bright smile. "Mrs. Hollister?"

"Yes?"

"How are you this afternoon? I'm here to check your mother's temp and blood pressure."

"Can it wait? She just drifted off to sleep a few minutes ago."

"No, I'm sorry. Doctor's orders."

She walked over to the bed and stood staring down at the sleeping woman. Audrey rose to join her.

"Are you new?" she asked, glancing at the woman's name tag. "I thought I'd met all the nurses in this wing, but I don't think I've ever seen you before."

"I'm Connie. I usually work on Three, but they were short-handed up here today so I'm filling in." She took down the blood pressure cuff from the wall over the bed. "Would you like to take a little breather while I'm in here? Go get some fresh air or a bite to eat?"

"I don't think so. When Mother wakes up, she'll be concerned if I'm not here," Audrey said.

"I'll stay with her till you get back. I know how it is when you've got family in the hospital. If you're not careful, you can get worn out and end up in here yourself. That wouldn't be good for anybody."

Audrey hesitated, but the offer was too tempting. "If you're sure you don't mind, I'll just run down and grab a snack in the cafeteria and bring it back up."

"Take your time," Connie said as she fiddled with the cuff. "We'll be just fine until you get back."

Audrey grabbed her purse and hurried out. As she headed down the hallway toward the elevators, she saw one of the nurses who usually took care of her mother behind the desk. She started to stop and explain where she was headed, but the woman looked harried and Audrey remembered what Connie had said about the floor being short-handed. She wouldn't bother the busy woman. Besides, she'd only be gone a few moments and Connie had promised to stay with her mother until she got back.

Although now that Audrey had left the room, something about the new nurse kept niggling at her, but she couldn't for the life of her figure out what it was.

The elevator stopped and as the doors slid open, two nurses got off. They were dressed in the usual scrubs, and as Audrey moved passed them to get on the elevator, she saw a name tag out of the corner of her eye.

She got on the elevator and pressed the button for the lobby level. Just as the doors started to close, a man stepped quickly through. He was tall and muscular, with long, dark hair pulled back into a ponytail. He nodded and smiled, then stood with one shoulder leaning against the wall of the elevator as they began to descend.

Audrey stared straight ahead, uneasy for some reason that she didn't understand. And then it hit her. She suddenly knew what had been nagging at her ever since she'd left her mother's room.

Connie's name tag. It was different from the ones the other nurses wore.

ELLIE HOLLISTER had just walked in the door when the phone started ringing. She grabbed the cordless unit off the island as she walked through the kitchen and headed into the living room where she could glance out the front window.

When she'd left earlier for her doctor's appointment, she'd noticed a dark-colored sedan parked at the curb in front of Mrs. Donley's house two doors down. She'd seen it there yesterday, too, when she'd gone to the grocery store and later when she'd picked Caitlin up from kindergarten.

Normally, she wouldn't have thought much about it except she knew Mrs. Donley was out of town visiting her daughter in Phoenix. It was possible the car belonged to another neighbor, but it wasn't the sort of vehicle that most of the young families in the upscale neighborhood drove.

Ellie had the phone to her ear as she pulled back the drapes and glanced out. "Hello?"

"Mrs. Hollister?"

"Yes?"

"Are you Ashley's mother?"

The question, along with the formal tone of the caller's voice, sent a chill of fear down Ellie's spine. *Oh, dear God...*

"Yes, I'm her mother. Has something happened? Is she okay?"

"There's been an incident at school."

The first thing that went through Ellie's mind was a school shooting. She sat down weakly in the nearest chair. "What kind of incident? Please, just tell me if my daughter's all right."

"She's not hurt, but the situation is serious. However I'd prefer to discuss it with you in person. How soon can you get here?"

"I'll be there in ten minutes."

"Please come to the principal's office when you arrive. We'll be waiting."

Ellie felt almost dizzy with relief. Ashley was okay. She wasn't hurt. For a moment, that was all that mattered.

And then it hit her. Something had happened at

school involving her daughter. Ashley was a little re-
bellious, but she was a good kid. Not the kind to stir
up trouble. Ellie had never gotten this kind of phone
call before.

Something else occurred to her as she got into her
car and backed out of the driveway. The caller had
never identified himself.

As she drove by Mrs. Donley's house, the dark
sedan pulled away from the curb behind her.

It was the afternoon recess at Fair Haven Academy, and
five-year-old Caitlin Hollister was playing on the jungle
gym with her best friend when Miss Allie, the substitute kindergarten teacher, came and told her that she had
to go back inside because her mother was on the phone.

"Is she sick?" Caitlin asked worriedly.

"No, no, I'm sure everything is fine. Nothing at
all for you to worry about." The pretty teacher smiled
and held out her hand. "Come on, sweetie. I'll walk
you inside."

Caitlin scrambled down off the jungle gym and
placed her hand inside Miss Allie's. Together they
walked back inside the building and down the long,
quiet corridor toward the offices.

They were about halfway down the hallway when
Caitlin wrinkled her nose and glanced around. "It
smells funny in here."

"What?" Miss Allie paused and sniffed the air.
"You're right. I smell it, too. Kind of like rotten eggs."

At that moment, they both saw the smoke. It seemed to come from nowhere, a thick cloud that rolled down the hallway toward them.

Caitlin's eyes burned and she started to cough. She couldn't stop. Still clutching her hand, Miss Allie whirled, but the smoke was coming from the other end of the hallway, too.

Pulling her shirt over her noise and mouth, the teacher tugged on Caitlin's hand. Instead of rushing back down the hallway toward the door they'd used earlier, she pulled Caitlin into one of the empty classrooms and closed the door.

Caitlin had never been so scared in her life. Tears streamed down her face, and her chest ached from the smoke. She clung to the teacher's hand, terrified to let her go.

But Miss Allie shook her off and headed toward the windows. When she couldn't get any of them open, she took a chair and smashed it against the glass. She kept at it until she had all the glass knocked out, and then she motioned for Caitlin. Picking her up, she helped Caitlin through the broken window, then climbed out behind her.

Still coughing, Miss Allie grabbed Caitlin's hand and started running away from the building. Caitlin ran, too, as fast as her legs would carry her. She could hear sirens and screams, but the sounds were distant, on the other side of the building. All Caitlin wanted to do was go find her mother, but instead of running toward those sounds, Miss Allie pulled her away from them.

They ran to the back of the building where a chain-link fence separated school property from a narrow, shady street. A car was parked just outside the fence, and as they neared the gate, a man got out and came toward them.

Caitlin stopped running. She tried to pull her hand free, but the teacher's grip tightened and she wouldn't let her go. Not even when Caitlin started to cry.

Chapter Ten

Cell phone pressed to his ear, Special Agent Pinson gave the kind of monosyllabic responses that wouldn't allow Graham to interpret the one-sided conversation.

"Was that Heller?" he asked when the agent finally ended the call. "What's going on with my family?"

"Heller will fill you in as soon as we get back to the office."

"Tell me now," Graham said through clenched teeth. "What the hell is going on?"

Pinson hesitated. "It may not be anything…"

Fear clawed at Graham's lungs. "What happened?"

"It's your niece, Caitlin. There was a fire at her school."

Graham's chest felt ready to explode. "Is she… how bad is it?"

"We don't know yet," the agent said, not taking his eyes from the road. "We haven't been able to find her. She and her teacher are missing."

WHEN Graham and Pinson walked into Heller's office, he was just getting off the phone. There were two other agents in the room, but they got up and left, nodding at Graham on their way out.

"Your niece is fine," Heller said before Graham could question him. "It was just a miscommunication on the ground. The thick smoke in the hallway created a lot of confusion, and the substitute teacher panicked and took Caitlin out through a window. That's why no one could find her, including our agent. She's fine, Graham. Everyone in your family is safe."

Graham sat down weakly in the chair opposite Heller's desk. "How could something like that happen? You said my whole family was under surveillance."

"They are. Everything is under control."

"Under control?" Graham asked in disbelief. "A fire breaks out in my niece's school, no one is able to find her and you call that under control?"

"There was no fire. Several smoke bombs were set off in the hallway. The children, including your niece, were never in any real danger."

"Who set them off?" Graham asked.

"We're looking into it. But let me stress again that no one in your family was in any real danger. We have agents watching your brother's home, his office, his daughters' schools, and your grandmother's hospital room. Everything is under control."

"I want to talk to my family," Graham said. "I want to make sure they're okay."

Heller nodded. "I understand. But we need to debrief you first. If Esteban knows about our involvement, then we may have a leak."

"What do you mean *if?* I told you about his phone call."

"Yes, and as I said earlier, he could have been bluffing. The guy in the restaurant wasn't one of our agents. It's possible that you confirmed to Esteban what may have been nothing more than guesswork on his part."

Graham's stomach roiled sickeningly. What had he done?

"No, wait a minute," he said slowly. "I didn't confirm anything. All I said was that I had the money. I'd do whatever he asked."

"Then here is my next question." Heller folded his hands on his desk and leaned forward. "If it wasn't a bluff, how did he know? How *could* he know, unless someone told him? Someone you know may be working against you, Graham. Who have you talked to about this?"

"No one."

"Not even Michael Barron?"

Graham hesitated, wondering if *Heller* was bluffing.

"What did the two of you talk about yesterday?"

So he *was* being watched. Graham didn't like this. Not one bit.

"Did you tell Michael Barron about the kidnapping?" Heller pressed. When Graham still said nothing, the agent frowned. "We've just established that someone close to you could be feeding Esteban information. I would think, under the circumstances, you would want to be a little more cooperative. So let's try this again. Did you talk to Barron about the kidnapping? Yes or no."

"Yes. I wanted to talk to someone I could trust," Graham said pointedly.

"How well do you know Barron?"

"He's been my best friend for years. We went to college together. He's like a brother to me. I'd trust him with my life."

"You may have done exactly that," Heller said with grim satisfaction. "How well does your wife know Mr. Barron?"

There was a strange glint in the agent's eyes that Graham didn't like.

"Like I said, he's my best friend so she's known him for years."

"Did you know she went to see him at his town house on the day of the reception? Did either of them tell you about that meeting?"

Graham swallowed. "No."

"Have you ever seen these photos before?"

Heller pushed a folder across the desk toward Graham. He hesitated a long moment before opening the file. The photographs inside had been taken from a distance, probably with a telephoto lens. They were of Michael and Kendall embracing, kissing, making love…

It took him a moment to realize the photographs were from before the accident, before Kendall's appearance had changed so drastically. But it didn't matter. Graham was stunned, blindsided. He closed the folder with a trembling hand.

"You didn't know about the affair?"

Graham's gaze shot up at the sound of Heller's voice. "Where did you get these?"

"Barron's ex-wife. That's why she left him. You didn't know about that, either, I suppose."

"I haven't seen Trish in years. Why would you talk to her about Kendall's kidnapping?"

"Because we don't think you're a random target. We've suspected from the start that someone close to you is working with the kidnappers."

"And you think that person is Michael? Have you talked to him?"

"Not yet. We wanted to talk to you first."

"Why?"

"Because some things still don't add up for us, Mr. Hollister." Heller's voice had cooled, and he was no longer on a first-name basis. Graham figured that probably wasn't a good sign. "We're hoping you can help us out."

"With what?"

"We find it a little strange that no one remembers

seeing your wife at the reception the night the ambassador was shot."

"What are you talking about? Dozens of people saw her there. We came in together."

"Your brother and sister-in-law didn't see her. And when we showed her picture to some of the other guests, none of them could say definitively that the woman they remembered in the red dress at the reception was the same person in the photograph."

Graham thought about that for a moment, and he recalled how Kendall had gone to freshen up when they came down from the roof. She hadn't come back for a very long time. "What about surveillance cameras or the guard who signed us in?"

"You were seen with a woman in a red dress. But the funny thing is…she always seemed to have her face turned away from the cameras. And the guard… well, he's just disappeared altogether."

Graham was silent for a moment as he tried to quell his fear. Whatever else he'd done, Michael had been right about this. The feds were trying to pin something on him. Only now it seemed as if Michael might be working against him, too.

And Kendall?

Graham glanced away and drew a long breath. All the lies were getting to him. Especially from the people he'd trusted the most.

His gaze jerked back to Heller as he forced himself to concentrate. "Am I a suspect?"

"In what?" Heller asked innocently.

"You seem to be suggesting that I might have had something to do with my wife's kidnapping."

"I'm not suggesting anything. I'm just thinking out loud. A man with your means finds out his wife has been having a five-year affair with his best friend. He confronts her, things get out of hand, he goes a little crazy and maybe he concocts a kidnapping story to cover up another crime."

Graham gripped the arms of his chair. "You're out of your mind."

"Did you know your wife has a record? She was arrested on a DUI charge back in college. Her fingerprints are in the system." Heller's eyes hardened as he leaned forward. "Her fingerprints are in the system, but they're nowhere to be found in your hotel suite."

Graham opened his mouth, but he had no idea what he was about to say.

Heller said it for him. "If you're about to suggest that the room has been cleaned, let me assure you that we found plenty of other prints. Yours. The maid's. Dozens of others we can't identify. But not your wife's. Not even on items that would have been used by her exclusively. Her lipstick. Hairbrush, toothbrush."

Graham shook his head. "That's impossible."

"So you can't explain the absence of your wife's fingerprints in the hotel suite you supposedly shared with her. You can't explain why no one can positively identify the woman in the red dress that you brought to the reception. You can't explain why—so far at least—the threats to your family haven't been carried out."

Graham was in a full-blown panic by now, but he managed to keep his voice low and even as he looked Heller in the eyes. "I'm not saying anything else until I've contacted my attorney."

"If you mean Mr. Barron, we'd like to have a word with him as well. Unfortunately, we haven't been able to reach him. But I don't suppose you know anything about that, either."

Graham rose. His legs were shaking, but he managed not to make a complete fool of himself. "Am I free to go?"

The question seemed to catch Heller off guard. "We're not done here."

"Let me put it another way then. Am I under arrest?"

Heller hesitated, then shrugged. "No."

"Then I'm outta here."

GRAHAM didn't know where else to go, so he headed back toward his office. As he walked along, he couldn't help reflecting on the near absurdity of the situation—he had two million dollars in his briefcase, he was a suspect in his own wife's kidnapping and no one on the street paid him the slightest bit of attention.

Once he got back to his building, he decided against going inside. Instead, he crossed the street and entered the parking garage. Opening the door of his car, he tossed in the briefcase and slid behind the wheel, still with no clue where he was going or what he should do.

He felt numb at the moment, but he knew that he was also on the verge of losing control.

Kendall and Michael…

He couldn't let himself think about that now. He had to keep his cool, figure a way out of all this.

Esteban had done a real number on him, maybe with the help of Graham's best friend. But he couldn't dwell on that right now, either. Not until he was someplace safe, where he could think. Where he could break down if he needed to and no one would see him, be able to use the lapse against him. Because, at the moment, he felt that his every move was being monitored and analyzed by both sides of the law.

Pulling out of the garage, he merged with the heavy downtown traffic. He still hadn't made any conscious decision about his destination, but a few minutes later, he found himself on the outskirts of the city, heading toward home.

He wondered if Agent Jones would still be in the house or if he would have already packed up and left now that Heller suspected Graham of masterminding Kendall's kidnapping.

Her fingerprints hadn't been found in their hotel suite. The only possible explanation was that Esteban had had them removed, but how could hers be cleaned away without disturbing the others? It made no sense.

And why couldn't anyone place her at the reception that night? She'd worn red, for God's sake. Her dress alone would have made her stand out.

Although, according to Heller, people remembered the dress but not the woman. Graham didn't understand that. Kendall was still very attractive. She got noticed wherever she went.

Unless for some reason she'd made a point of *not* getting noticed. If she had deliberately stayed away from the crowd until the last possible moment…

What was it Heller had said about the security tapes? Kendall's face was always turned.

Graham hated the direction of his thoughts, but he couldn't run away from this. He couldn't hide from his suspicions.

He hated that the FBI considered him a suspect, but he despised even more his growing doubts about his own wife. Five years ago she'd had an affair with his best friend. Graham had seen the evidence with his own two eyes.

Had the affair continued? Were Kendall and Michael in this together somehow?

What if they'd engineered the whole thing to extort money from him?

His fingers tightened on the steering wheel. *Stop it!* Kendall would never do something like that. She loved him. She was committed to him. Whatever she'd had with Michael was over.

But it wasn't over. Because Graham had just

found out about it, and it didn't matter that five years had gone by. It didn't matter that Kendall had changed. That *he* had changed. She'd cheated on him with his best friend. That wasn't something Graham could forgive or forget. Not now. Maybe not ever.

In spite of everything he'd just learned, though, his resolve to find her hadn't lessened. He wanted her back. He wanted her safe.

And then he would deal with the rest. Somehow.

HE WAS only a few miles from home when Esteban's phone rang. Glancing in his rearview mirror, Graham lifted it to his ear.

"Pull over," a voice told him.

"I'm on the highway. There's no safe place to stop the car."

"We know where you are, Mr. Hollister. Find a place and pull over."

Graham glanced in his mirror again, then putting on his blinker, he slowed and eased the car to the shoulder of the road.

"Okay, I'm off the road."

"Turn off the ignition and take out the key."

Graham complied. "What now?"

"Get out of the car."

His heart thudded against his ribcage as he opened the door and climbed out, his gaze immediately scanning the highway and the woods behind him. Was he about to be ambushed?

"As soon as I hang up, I want you to go to the back of the car and open the trunk."

"Why?"

The call ended and Graham snapped the phone shut and slipped it into his pocket as he walked to the rear of the car.

He gazed around. The afternoon traffic on the highway was getting heavy. He could feel the tug of the rushing air as a steady stream of cars flowed past him.

Using his remote, he popped the trunk but he didn't immediately lift the lid. Part of him wanted just to leave it closed and run because he knew something bad was about to happen. He could feel it in his gut.

He stood that way for a long moment until a horn sounded and he jumped. The car swished by without slowing.

Graham turned back to the trunk. He waited for a gap in the traffic, then threw up the lid.

The first thing that hit him was the smell of blood. His hand flew over his mouth and nose as he stared down into the trunk.

Michael's sightless eyes stared up at him.

Chapter Eleven

Michael's face was ashen, his dark hair matted with blood from the entry and exit bullet holes in his forehead and at the back of his skull. His arms had been pulled back and fastened behind his back.

He had been executed.

Bile rose in Graham's throat, and for a moment, he could hardly comprehend what he was seeing. His first coherent thought was that he had to get help. He had to call an ambulance and the police.

But he almost immediately realized that an ambulance wouldn't be necessary. Michael was dead. There was no mistaking that.

And if he called the police, he would be their number-one suspect. He could be arrested, detained for days. What would happen to Kendall? And to his family? He certainly couldn't rely on the FBI to protect them. He was their number-one suspect, too.

Slamming down the trunk, Graham stumbled to the side of the car and climbed back inside. He turned the air conditioner on, positioning the vents so the cold air blew directly on his face.

He felt weak and dizzy and too overwhelmed to contemplate what he should do. All he could think about at the moment was Michael, dead in his trunk. He'd been murdered in cold blood for no other reason than to prove a point to Graham.

Wiping a shaking hand across his mouth, he closed his eyes in disbelief.

The phone in his pocket started ringing. He pulled it out and lifted it to his ear.

"Mr. Hollister?"

Still he said nothing.

"I understand. You must be in shock." The note of false sympathy infuriated Graham. His hand tightened on the phone.

"You son of a bitch."

"Call me what you like, but what happened to Michael Barron is your fault. I warned you not to go to the authorities. I warned you there would be consequences if you didn't follow the rules. Now you know that I mean exactly what I say."

Graham glanced out the window as a truck sped by on the highway. His car swayed in the aftermath, and he thought fleetingly that he needed to get off the side of the road. It wasn't safe with all the traffic.

Safe.

The concept was almost laughable, considering.

Michael was dead, stuffed in his trunk, and somehow Graham had to keep it together.

"That could just as easily be your mother or brother or niece in the trunk. Everyone in your family is vulnerable. And if you think the FBI can protect them, you are very much mistaken. Break another rule, and the fire at your niece's school will be real next time."

Graham put a hand on the steering wheel and clutched it. "You touch her and I'll kill you."

Esteban laughed. "You're hardly in any position to make threats. You brought the FBI into the game, Mr. Hollister, and now I'm taking them out. It's only a matter of time before they find the gun used to kill Michael Barron on your property, along with other evidence that will seal your fate."

"They'll never believe it," Graham said, but he knew that wasn't true. Heller already suspected him of engineering Kendall's kidnapping to cover up her disappearance. Michael's murder would fit all too neatly into their preconceived scenario.

"Oh, we both know they'll believe it," Esteban said. "It ties up everything very neatly for them so, of course, they'll believe it. A warrant will be issued for your arrest. You'll become a fugitive, a wanted man, but if you ever want to see your wife again, you'll have to find a way to evade capture. If you can't meet my demands, your wife goes away forever."

"What do you want me to do?"

"Do you still have the money?"

"Yes."

"The price is now seven million. You have twenty-four hours."

Graham was starting to get a chill from the air conditioning, but he didn't dare turn it off. The cold air kept him alert. "I can't raise another five million overnight. I need more time."

"You have twenty-four hours."

"I'm telling you, it's impossible! I can't lay my hands on that much money that quickly."

"Perhaps not, but your brother can. He received a check for roughly that amount from the sale of your father's ranch. The transaction took place this morning. The money should still be readily available in his account."

"How do you know about that?"

"There is one other thing that we need from you, Mr. Hollister."

"What?" What else could they possible want from him?

"We need a complete set of blueprints for the PemCo Tower."

Graham sat stunned.

"Did you hear me, Mr. Hollister? Bring the blueprints to Houston and await my phone call."

"No."

There was silence on the other end. "You refuse? Then you leave me no choice. I have a man watching your brother's house right now. Your niece is playing in the backyard. Would you like to know what is about to happen to her?"

The call ended and Graham started to tremble. What had he done?

The phone rang again and he snatched it up instantly. No one said anything, but he could hear a child's laughter in the background. Then the phone went dead again.

He waited in dread. The phone rang again and he said desperately, "Okay. You win. I'll do whatever you say. Just don't hurt her."

"The clock is ticking, Mr. Hollister. If I were you, I would not waste time talking. You should probably take care of business in Austin, and then get to Houston before the police issue an APB on your car."

GRAHAM caught the tail end of rush hour as he drove into Houston. The westbound lanes of 290 were stop-and-go, but thankfully he was going against the traffic. Heading into downtown, however, the streets and interstates were still heavily congested.

He found a seedy motel on the south side of town and paid for two nights in cash. Then he drove around to the back and parked so that his car couldn't be seen from the street.

Taking the briefcase and blueprints with him, he got out, locked the car and walked away. He didn't even go inside the room, but instead headed down the street to a pay phone he'd spotted earlier.

It was after six, but Graham hoped to catch Terrence at the office rather than home. He didn't want to talk to Ellie just yet. The guilt he felt over what had happened to Caitlin was still too raw, and he couldn't let himself think about that right now, either.

Terrence's assistant, Evelyn Fletcher, answered the phone. Graham had known Evelyn for years. In her early sixties, she'd been his father's personal assistant for nearly thirty years, right up until his death, and then she'd stayed on to work for Terrence. She was like part of the family, and she knew more about the business than just about anyone.

She seemed surprised to hear Graham's voice, and he supposed it was little wonder. He could count on one hand the number of times he'd called Terrence at work in the past few years.

"You just caught him," she said when Graham asked if his brother was in. "We were both about to call it a day."

"I need a favor," Graham said. "And it's probably going to sound a little strange."

"What is it?" Her tone grew concerned. "Is everything okay?"

"It will be, but I need to talk to Terrence. And I need to make sure that no one else knows about this call."

Evelyn hesitated. "Does this have something to do with the FBI coming around yesterday asking questions about Kendall?" She lowered her voice, and

Graham could imagine her surreptitious glance around the office. Evelyn was nobody's fool. She had to know something was going on.

"I can't explain it right now. But I need you to give Terrence a message for me. Have him call me back at the number I'm about to give you, but not from the phone in his office. Not from his cell phone, either."

"Graham, what on earth is going on?" she asked worriedly.

"I'm sorry, Evelyn. I hate involving you in this, but I need your help. And I need you not to ask any more questions. Will you give Terrence the message?"

"Of course I will. You know I'd do anything to help you out. You and Terrence are family."

"Thanks. You don't know how much I appreciate that," Graham said. "Write this number on a piece of paper and hand it to Terrence. And don't repeat it back when I give it to you. Understand?"

"Yes, but, Graham…I wish your father was still alive. If you're in some sort of trouble, he'd know what to do."

"It'll be all right. Just give Terrence this number."

Graham finished the call and hung up. Evelyn was wrong, he thought. Even Nate Hollister wouldn't have been able to get him out of this mess.

AN HOUR LATER, Terrence arrived at the restaurant where they'd agreed to meet. Graham had a booth by the window so he could watch the parking lot and the front door.

He didn't recognize his brother when he first drove up. Terrence was driving an unfamiliar car for one thing, and for another, he had on a baseball cap and sunglasses. Not exactly his brother's usual attire.

As soon as he entered the restaurant, the cap came off. A moment later, he slid into the booth across from Graham.

"You weren't followed?" he asked anxiously.

"No."

"Are you sure?"

"I left through the warehouse side door like you suggested. You can't see it from the street or the parking lot. If anyone was watching the building they wouldn't have seen me."

"What about the car?"

"It's Evelyn's daughter's car. She drove it to work today because hers is in the shop." Terrence took off the sunglasses and laid them aside. "Are you going to tell me what's going on?"

Graham glanced out the window, his gaze automatically sweeping the parking lot. "I don't even know where to start."

"How about with the two FBI agents that barged into my office yesterday morning asking questions about your relationship with Kendall? I thought at first it was just a routine interview. They were checking out everyone who had been at the reception.

But it was more than that, wasn't it? It didn't have anything to do with the ambassador's shooting. What do they think they have on you, Graham?"

He gave their surroundings a quick scan. "They think I had something to do with Kendall's kidnapping."

"Her *kidnapping?*" Terrence said in shock. "What the hell are you talking about?"

"She disappeared from the reception the other night. She called later and asked me to meet her at home. When I got back to Austin, four armed men broke into the house and told me that she'd been kidnapped. And unless I followed their rules, I'd never see her again."

Terrence stared at him in disbelief. "Why didn't you tell me about this earlier? Maybe I could have done something."

In spite of the situation, his tone annoyed Graham. "What could you have done? These guys are killers, Terrence. Cold-blooded murderers."

"How do you know that?"

Graham glanced away, took a moment to draw a breath, then brought his eyes back to Terrence. "Because they killed Michael."

He could see Terrence's mind working, trying to process the information. "No. That's not possible. I saw Michael this morning. He came into my office and said he had some personal business to take care of. He was going to be out for the rest of the day…"

The realization that he hadn't seen Michael in hours hit him. "Graham, how do you know—"

"Because I saw him," Graham said. "He was shot."

Terrence stared at him for a long moment. "Where?"

"I don't know where he was killed, but they put his body in the trunk of my car. As far as I know, it's still there."

A waitress ambled toward their table, but Terrence waved her away. For the longest moment, neither of them spoke.

Then Terrence abruptly stood. "We need to get out of here. This isn't a good place for a conversation like this."

He threw some bills on the table and Graham followed him out. They got in the borrowed car and Terrence started the ignition while Graham stored the briefcase and blueprints in the backseat.

"Where are we going?" he asked.

Terrence shrugged. "Damned if I know. But just give me a few minutes, okay? Don't say anything else until I have time to get my head around this."

TERRENCE drove around aimlessly for a few minutes before finally pulling into the parking lot of a huge discount store. He parked at the back, away from the other cars, and shut off the ignition.

"Are you sure Michael is dead?" he finally said.

"Hell, yes, I'm sure."

"There's no chance you could be mistaken?" His

tone was strained, but calm. "Do we need to go back and make sure?"

"He's dead, Terrence. There's no mistake."

"And you think the people who kidnapped Kendall are responsible? Why would they kill Michael?"

"Because I broke one of their rules. I went to the FBI after they warned me not to."

"So why kill Michael?"

"Maybe because he was an easy target. And they couldn't get to anyone else. You and Ellie and the girls have been under FBI surveillance since this happened. So have Mom and Gran."

Terrence's eyes turned cold as he stared at Graham. "What?"

"You've all been under FBI protection because the threat included my whole family," Graham said.

Terrence exploded in fury. "Damn it, Graham, and you didn't tell me about this? How could you keep it from me?"

He shrugged in helpless frustration. "I wanted to tell you. I knew you had a right to know. But Heller, the agent in charge of the investigation, said it would put the family in even more danger if a change in routine tipped off the kidnappers. Heller promised me they would keep you all safe. But now I know that he can't keep that promise. Esteban proved that today."

Terrence turned. "You mean Michael?"

"That…and other things."

Comprehension dawned on his brother's face and

he swore. "The false alarm at Caitlin's school today. That was this guy…what did you call him? Esteban?"

Graham nodded.

Terrence rubbed a hand across his mouth. "That wasn't the only thing that happened. Ellie received a strange phone call today from Ashley's school. She was told there had been some kind of incident, but when she got to the principal's office, no one knew anything about it. Ashley was fine. That call had something to do with this, too, didn't it?"

"I don't know." Graham hadn't known about the phone call, but he had no doubt Esteban was behind it. He'd coordinated both incidents to prove how truly vulnerable Graham's family was. "Have you talked to Mom today?"

"A couple of hours ago. She and Gran are both fine."

But for how long? How the hell was Graham supposed to protect his family when he might not even be able to stay out of jail?

He could feel Terrence's eyes on him, and he glanced up. "I'm sorry. I should have told you sooner. I thought I was doing the right thing. I thought I could trust the FBI to protect you and Ellie and the girls. And Mom and Gran. But they can't protect any of us. And now I don't think they'll even try."

Terrence frowned. "What do you mean?"

"They think I did it, Terrence. They think I engineered Kendall's kidnapping to cover up another crime. And as soon as they find out about Michael, I'll be arrested for his murder."

"Why the hell would they think you killed Michael? He was your best friend. He was like a brother to you. You were closer to him than you are to me."

What was that strange little edge in Terrence's voice? Anger? Fear? Bitterness?

"They'll believe it because I have a motive. The oldest one in the book. Michael and Kendall had an affair five years ago. The FBI has proof."

"What proof?"

"Trish gave them photographs. Evidently she suspected Michael was cheating and she hired a private detective. When she found out about the affair, she left him."

"So that was the reason they split up. I always wondered," Terrence murmured.

Graham glanced at his brother. "You didn't know? About Michael and Kendall, I mean."

"Of course I didn't know," he said angrily. "You think I would have kept something like that from you? I'm your brother, for God's sake."

"You never told me about L. J. Kittering."

Guilt sparked in Terrence's eyes before he glanced away. "That was different. You and Kendall were separated at the time. I thought you were getting a divorce. I didn't think it mattered. I didn't think you would even care. Then after the accident, when you got back together, I didn't see the point in bringing it up. You were happy. I didn't want to be the one to spoil it for you."

"But you had your doubts about the reconciliation. You never liked Kendall, did you?"

Terrence shrugged. "Maybe not back then. But she changed after the accident. At least…it seemed so." He paused, staring pensively out the windshield. "I'm sorry, Graham, but I have to ask this. Are you sure Kendall isn't somehow involved in all this?"

Graham wasn't sure of anything anymore. Two days ago, he would have sworn that the woman he'd lived with for the past five years would never betray him. Never hurt him. Now he had no idea who she was or what in his life was even real.

"I don't know," he said truthfully. "All I know is that I have to find her."

"Where do I come in?"

"I need help with the ransom."

"How much do they want?"

"Seven million. I have two million and less than twenty-four hours to raise the rest."

Terrence glanced at his watch. "The banks are closed. I won't be able to do anything until tomorrow morning."

"You'll help me then? In spite of everything I've told you."

"Like I said, you're my brother. I may not agree with how you've handled things, but I don't know that I would have done it any differently if I were in your shoes. To tell you the truth, I don't know how you're holding up as well as you are after everything you've been through."

Graham started to turn away, then stopped. His emotions were raw and on the surface, but he suddenly didn't care if his brother witnessed his vulnerability. The differences they'd had in the past seemed petty and inconsequential.

He drew a long breath. "I have to get her back, Terry."

"I know," Terrence said gruffly. "But this guy Esteban…he's not going to let up. You give him the money and he'll keep squeezing until he's wrung every drop he can out of you. There's nothing to keep him from coming back time and again."

"That won't happen," Graham said grimly. "Once Kendall is safe, I'm going to kill him."

It wasn't bravado, but a statement of fact and Terrence seemed to accept it as such. If he was surprised or alarmed, he didn't show it. Instead he said slowly, "I may know someone who can help us."

Us. Graham swallowed. "Who?"

"Do you remember a guy named Walter Clarkson? He was an old army buddy of Dad's. They served in Korea together. He used to tell me every time I saw him how Dad had saved his life. He named his son after him. Nathan was military, too. Special Forces. A real badass, from what Dad said. After he left the service, he worked in intelligence for a while.

I never knew any of the details, but a few years ago, he went solo."

"Meaning?"

"He's a hired gun now. The type of guy you call when the police can't fix your problem."

"And you know this how?"

"Not through personal experience, thank God. Evelyn's daughter was being stalked a few years back. The police couldn't do anything about it so Dad called Walter and he put him in touch with his son. The stalking stopped almost immediately."

"What did he do?"

"I don't know and I don't care. The point is, Dad gave me his number in case I ever needed it. I think the incident with Evelyn's daughter shook him up, and he was worried that something like that might someday happen to one of my girls."

"You've still got the number?"

"I dug it out as soon as the FBI left my office. We need to talk to him, Graham. The sooner the better, if you ask me."

Chapter Twelve

Terrence made arrangements for Graham to meet with Nathan Clarkson that night at an abandoned farmhouse in Waller County, a rural, wooded community north of Houston. Graham hadn't spoken to Clarkson personally, nor had he ever met the man. He knew nothing about him other than the scant information Terrence had provided. That their fathers had once been army buddies was hardly a ringing endorsement, and Graham wasn't particularly in a trusting mood these days.

But he didn't see that he had much of a choice. With the FBI out of the equation, he was on his own. And even though the brutality of the past few days had opened Graham's eyes, he knew he wasn't equipped to deal with the situation that faced him. There was a reason Esteban wanted the plans to the PemCo Tower. And it wasn't a good one.

If Graham wanted to stop Esteban for good, he had to have help. He had to have someone on his side who knew how to operate in Esteban's world.

After the call to Clarkson, Terrence had taken a cab back to the office, leaving Graham with Evelyn's borrowed car. He'd driven to another parking lot, found an inconspicuous spot and tried to catch some sleep. He'd managed to doze off a couple of times, but every little noise awakened him with a start. He'd finally given up, turned on the radio and sat listening to music as he thought about Kendall, wondering how she was holding up.

What he didn't let himself think about was the affair. Or what he would say to her when he saw her again. None of that could matter at the moment, not while lives were still in danger. He couldn't afford to focus on anything but stopping Esteban. He would deal with the rest later.

Backing the car down the gravel drive in front of the farmhouse, Graham turned off the engine and killed the headlights. He'd gotten to the meeting place ahead of Clarkson, and now he watched the road. He lowered his window so that he could hear an approaching vehicle before he could see it through the trees. In spite of his exhaustion, he was alert and wired, anxious to hear what Clarkson had to say.

Even though he was expecting Clarkson, the sound of a car engine sent a spurt of adrenaline through his veins and his heart started to pound. A moment later, headlights pulled into the drive, and Graham squinted in the glare.

The lights didn't go off. It was almost as if

Clarkson was waiting for Graham to make the first move. After a moment of indecision, Graham opened the door and got out. He walked around to the front of the car and stood in the headlight beam. He started to put his arms up to show that he didn't have a weapon, but the action made him feel foolish and he dropped his hands to his sides.

A car door opened and a man got out. Slowly he walked into the light.

"Graham Hollister?"

"Yes."

"Nathan Clarkson." He held out his hand and the two men shook.

Graham had never seen Clarkson before and he hadn't known what to expect. After everything Terrence had told him about the man's background, Graham supposed he'd formed a vague Rambo-type image in his head that was immediately dispelled on meeting Nathan Clarkson face to face.

The man was neither short nor tall, not heavy or thin, but completely nondescript in every way. He was by nature and skill someone who blended into his surroundings without being noticed.

His brown hair was cut short and his wire-rimmed glasses gave him an earnest, boyish look despite the lines around his eyes and mouth.

He went quickly back to his car and shut off the lights. Then he nodded toward the sagging porch on the farmhouse. "Let's sit down."

They walked through the tall grass and sat on the top step. Graham leaned forward, forearms on his knees as he stared straight ahead into the darkness. It was a warm night, with fireflies flitting through the grass and frogs croaking from the ditches. He could hear an owl somewhere in the trees that surrounded the house. But other than the wildlife, the night was deadly silent.

"I chose this place for two reasons," Clarkson said. "If the kidnappers are using your cell phone to track you, they may decide that you've come out here to dispose of the body."

Graham flinched. "And if they don't?"

"I own this place. You can't tell by looking, but it's secure. If anyone comes within a couple of miles, we'll know about it."

That made Graham feel a little easier. Assuming, of course, that Clarkson wasn't just blowing smoke. "So what do we do?"

"The first thing I need to tell you is this. I'm an independent contractor. I don't work for the government, although I occasionally do work for the government." He shrugged. "Fine distinction, but there is one. I'm not limited by laws or international protocol. I do whatever it takes to get the job done. Are you comfortable with that?"

"Whatever it takes to get my wife back and keep my family safe. That's all I care about."

"That's easy enough to say, but when it comes

down to the dirty work, people like you tend to get a little squeamish."

"You don't know anything about me," Graham said angrily. "I got past squeamish when I found my best friend's body in the trunk of my car. I want this nightmare to be over. I want my life back."

Clarkson nodded. "Okay. We've got a few things to go over then. Terrence briefed me about the situation on the phone, but I'm going to need to hear it from you. I apologize for that because I know you've probably told it a dozen times or more by now. I still need to hear it. Start at the beginning and give me as many details as you can remember."

"All right. But I need to tell you something first that Terrence doesn't know anything about." Graham paused, his gaze on the flickering fireflies in the distance. "The kidnappers want more than just money. They want a set of plans to the PemCo Tower."

Clarkson was pensive for a moment. "Do you have the plans?"

"Yes. I drove back into Austin yesterday and got them. I don't know what Esteban has planned, but it can't be good."

"No, you're right about that," Clarkson said. "And it does put a whole new spin on things. But for now, let's concentrate on what we do know."

Graham gazed straight ahead as he told the story from beginning to end, stopping to elaborate when

Clarkson interrupted with a question. When he was finished, they both sat in silence.

"Have you handled this kind of situation before?" Graham finally asked.

"Kidnappings for ransom? Sure. But we're dealing with something different here. The amount of the ransom—seven million dollars—is nothing to these guys. By the sounds of the operation, that amount would barely cover their expenses."

"Then why bother?"

"The money is just a smokescreen. They threw out a number that they knew you would be able to come up with to test you."

"They wanted the plans all along. They're going to bomb that building, aren't they?"

"All we know for sure is that they've gone to a lot of trouble to put you in this position. I have a feeling everything will start happening pretty quickly from this point on. This guy Esteban has set you up to take the fall for Barron's murder, so he'll have to move fast before the police and FBI close in on you. I'd say you have a day at the most."

Graham's hands were sweating. He wiped them on the legs of his slacks.

"This kind of situation is about as scary as it gets," Clarkson said sympathetically. "And it'll get worse, believe me." He paused. "Tell me about Esteban. You said he has acne scars on his face. He's tall, dark, somewhere in his forties. Is there anything else you may have left out?"

Graham tried to think back, but the exhaustion was working against him now. His mind was cloudy, and he had a feeling he was leaving out important details. He described Esteban again, taking his time, hoping that something else would come back to him.

When he finished, he turned to Clarkson. "Have you ever heard of him?"

"Esteban. No, not the name. I'm sure it's an alias. But I've got a lot of contacts across the border. As soon as we're finished here, I'll start making some calls. With the description you gave me, it's possible we'll have identification within a matter of hours. Then it'll be a matter of determining whether he's flying solo. I don't think he is. He's got someone funding the operation, which is why the ransom money is not a big deal to him."

"What about Leo Kittering? Do you know anything about him?"

"Only by reputation."

"Do you think it's possible he could be funding Esteban?"

"Kittering's business is drugs. I've never heard of him being involved in kidnappings for ransom, and again, seven million dollars is chicken feed to a guy like him. If he's in this, it's something personal. A vendetta."

"Against my wife?"

"If he blames her for his son's death. I've already got someone watching Kittering's compound. If he's a part of this, it shouldn't be difficult to confirm. Bribes in that part of the world are a way of life."

"What about Kendall?"

"With a little luck, we may be able to find out where he's holding her."

Graham's heart skipped a beat. It was the first positive thing he'd heard since this whole nightmare started. "And then?"

"We go in and take her."

"That sounds dangerous."

"Not the way we handle extractions."

The matter-of-fact way he said it made Graham almost believe him.

"But even if we do find your wife, it won't end this," Clarkson said, dashing Graham's brief euphoria. "If Kittering and Esteban have formed an alliance, taking Kittering out of the equation won't stop Esteban. The only way to do that is to take him out. You need to understand that."

Graham nodded, knowing exactly what Clarkson meant by *take him out*. "Let's do it."

CLARKSON swapped vehicles with Graham, leaving him with a fresh cell phone and a card key to a motel room back in the city where he could get some rest that night. Clarkson also took the keys to Graham's

BMW so that arrangements could be made to dispose of Michael's body.

Graham was dead tired, and after showering, he wanted nothing more than to collapse in bed, close his eyes and shut everything out.

But as depleted as he was, it still took him a long time to fall asleep. A knock on the door awakened him with a start. His eyes flew open and he squinted at the light seeping through the closed drapes. It was morning. He'd slept for hours.

The knock became more insistent. Graham drew on his pants and went to the door. "Who is it?"

"Clarkson."

Graham snapped the deadbolt and drew back the chain lock. He opened the door and Clarkson pushed past him. He had on sunglasses which he whipped off as soon as he was inside.

He sat down at the small table and started pulling files and photos out of his briefcase. "Have a seat." He nodded toward the chair across from him. "We've got a lot to go over."

"Mind if I brush my teeth and wash my face first?"

Clarkson shrugged as he continued to dig through his briefcase. "Sure, go ahead. But don't take too long. Like I said, we've a lot to talk about and not much time."

Not much time. What did that mean? Graham wondered as he hurried into the bathroom to freshen up. A few minutes later, he came back out and grabbed his shirt from the back of a chair. Slipping it on, he buttoned it up as he took a seat.

Clarkson shoved a photograph across the table. "Is this your guy?"

Graham took one look and nodded. The shot was grainy and had been snapped from a great distance on a crowded street. But Esteban was facing the camera and there was no mistake. It was him.

"His real name is Gabriel Galindo. His mother was American, but he was raised in Mexico by his stepbrother after their father died. The brother's name is Joaquin Galindo. He was head of the oil workers' labor union in Mexico until he ended up in prison."

"I know who he is," Graham said. "He's thought to be responsible for the PemCo refinery explosion that killed all those people a couple of years back."

"PemCo's alliance with Petroleos Mexicanos—Pemex—has created a volatile situation. Do you know much about the oil situation in Mexico?"

Graham shook his head. "Not really. The industry is controlled by the state. That's about all I know."

"Since 1938, when Mexico first nationalized the oil industry, Pemex has been a sacred symbol of Mexico's sovereignty. The recent loosening of regulations allowing outside investors—PemCo being the largest—was viewed by some as the first step toward privatization and the exploitation of Mexico's vast petroleum resources by foreign oil companies.

"Protests erupted on both sides of the border, culminating in the refinery explosion you mentioned. Galindo had been arrested five years prior on weapons and murder charges and was serving a thirty-five-year jail sentence. But it is widely believed that the bombing was carried out under his orders."

"What does that have to do with the current situation?"

"If PemCo suffers enough losses, they could be forced to pull out of the alliance. It's possible Esteban wants to use this leverage to bargain for his brother's release. As the architect on the project, you've had unlimited access to the building. I wouldn't be surprised if Esteban has had you in his sights from the very beginning."

"What about Leo Kittering?"

"I'm guessing he paid Esteban to do what he couldn't—come across the border and get your wife. Esteban gets the funding he needs and Kittering gets his revenge."

Graham got up and started to pace. "How do we stop them?"

"As I said, Kittering's compound is being watched around the clock, and we've got a lead on where Kittering may be holding your wife."

Graham's heart thudded. "What kind of lead?"

"It looks promising, but we won't know for sure until I've put men inside the compound. As soon as my guys go in, the game changes. Without your wife or your family as bartering chips, Esteban will come after you with everything he's got. And make no mistake, it'll be a bloodbath."

Graham sat down at the table across from Clarkson. He wasn't sure what he was supposed to say to that. It all sounded like something from an action movie. But Graham was no hero. He wasn't any kind of hero. He was just a desperate man who wanted his life back.

Clarkson opened another folder and took out a photograph that he passed to Graham. This one was of a woman. Dark hair, late twenties, attractive.

"Have you ever seen this woman before?"

Graham shook his head. "No, who is she?"

"Her name is Nikki Singer. She used to be with the American consulate in Mexico City before she left to work for Leo Kittering."

Graham glanced up with a frown. "What's her connection to this?"

"Leo Kittering's son was found murdered in this woman's apartment. She disappeared that night and no one has heard from her since. The consulate tried to locate her, but she didn't leave a trail. If she came across the border, she did so under the radar."

"I still don't get what she has to do with any of this. Are you saying this woman killed Kittering's son? If that's the case, why would he come after Kendall?"

"He didn't. He came after Nikki Singer."

"What are you talking about?"

Clarkson nodded toward the photograph. "Take

another look. Are you sure you've never seen her before?"

Graham glanced down, started to dismiss the photograph impatiently, then froze. There was something about the woman's eyes. Not the shape or the color, but what was behind them. A haunted look he'd seen before…

His heart flailed wildly against his ribcage. For a moment, he couldn't tear his gaze from the woman's eyes, and then slowly he looked up.

Clarkson nodded. "It would explain why Kendall Hollister's fingerprints weren't found in your hotel suite, wouldn't it?"

It would explain a lot of other things, too, but Graham shook his head. "It's not possible."

Plastic surgery had changed Kendall's appearance. The near-death experience had altered her personality. And the gaps in her memory…the doctors had told him they were normal following a severe trauma. Everything was attributable to the accident. Of course Kendall had changed. So had he. But to suggest—

Graham flashed suddenly to the key taped to the bottom of the music box. The key to Kendall's past. Or was it Nikki Singer's past?

He glanced up from the photo. "I don't believe it. I would have known." But even as he denied it, Graham was assailed by doubt. The woman he'd been living with for the past five years was nothing like the woman he'd married.

"How could I not have seen it?" he murmured.

"The more important question is this. Does any of what I've told you this morning change our arrangement?"

Graham glanced back down at the photograph. Images flashed through his head. Kendall's smile. Her laugh. The touch of her hand.

The way she looked at him. The way she whispered his name in the dark. The way she moved beneath him...

He closed his eyes. "Just get her out of there. I don't know what happens after that, but I can't leave her down there, no matter who she is. Kittering will kill her." He couldn't have that on his conscience no matter what Nikki Singer had done to him.

And there was a chance that Clarkson was wrong about this.

There was a chance that the past five years of his life hadn't been a lie after all.

He rubbed a hand across his face. "If what you say is true, where's Kendall?" he asked. "Where's my wife?"

Clarkson's gaze met his. "My guess is, she's dead."

Chapter Thirteen

With Terrence's help, Graham had the rest of the ransom by two o'clock that afternoon, but it was after midnight before he received his next set of instructions. He was to bring the money and the plans to an alley behind a warehouse on Navigation.

The neighborhood had once been German, but was now predominantly Hispanic. The original Ninfa's restaurant was located in the area, along with a few artist's galleries and lofts that were cropping up in some of the warehouses.

Graham located the address and parked on the street. Getting out of the car, he grabbed the briefcase and plans from the back seat and slowly walked toward the dark alley. Before he'd gone more than a few feet, a van swung up next to him. The side door opened, and two men wearing ski masks jumped out.

One grabbed the briefcase and tubes while the other clipped him on the back of the head with his gun. Pain shot threw his skull and Graham's knees buckled.

Before he could hit the ground, he was shoved toward the van door. As he fell forward, hands reached from inside the vehicle and dragged him in. He landed with a hard thud on the metal floor. The door slid closed and the van backed out of the alley, then eased back onto the street.

Graham tried to sit up, but someone put a knee in the small of his back and pushed him back down. He was searched for weapons and a wire, and when nothing was found, his arms were pulled back and handcuffed behind him.

The pressure on his back eased as the knee lifted from his spine and he was rolled over. The men who had grabbed him still wore their ski masks as they knelt on either side of him.

"Check the tubes," one of them barked in Spanish.

While his partner checked the blueprints, the one who had spoken kept his eyes on Graham.

He tried to sit up, but the guy beside him didn't like that. He shoved him back to the floor. *"No mueve."* Don't move.

"Where are you taking me?"

"To see Esteban."

"Why? You have the plans. Why don't you let me go?"

The man said something in Spanish to the driver. The van slowed, made a quick turn, then picked up speed. Graham could see nothing from where he lay. He wasn't even sure how many men were in the van.

Three, for sure—the two that had grabbed him and the driver. He didn't know if someone rode in the passenger seat or not, but it didn't matter. The odds were against him, even if his hands hadn't been fastened behind his back.

The van stopped for a traffic light, and Graham turned his head to try and get a look out the window.

Suddenly, the side glass on the driver's side shattered and the man slumped over the wheel. The door opened and hands reached in to drag him out of the seat. He rolled out and landed on the street.

At the same time, the passenger door opened and another man jumped inside. "Nobody move," Clarkson ordered, aiming a gun toward the back of the van.

Graham had never been so glad to see anyone in his life.

Behind him, the man who had checked the blueprints went for his gun. Clarkson fired, and the guy's head flew back against the metal panel. He fell to the floor, eyes open but sightless.

Graham hadn't been prepared for that. A rush of adrenaline and terror made him feel light-headed and sick, but he tried to shake off the dizziness.

Having witnessed his comrades shot at point-blank range, the third man dropped his gun and put up his hands. While Clarkson climbed into the back and unfastened the handcuffs around Graham's wrists, the man who had shot the driver climbed behind the wheel. When the light changed, he drove calmly through the intersection.

"Now then," Clarkson said as he sat down on the floor, gun pointed at the third man's forehead. "Let's have a little chat, shall we? You can start by telling me where the hell we're going."

THE MAN'S name was Hector Reyes, he informed them, and he had been sent to act as a liaison between Esteban and Reyes's boss, Leo Kittering.

He hadn't been forthcoming with this or any other information at first, but Clarkson, as Graham soon discovered, was brutally persuasive. When they arrived at the PemCo Tower—the van's destination—Reyes's screams still echoed in Graham's ears.

After handcuffing the man to the van floor, Clarkson and his associate pulled on the ski masks and escorted Graham at gunpoint into the building. They were let in through a side door by a guard who said something to Clarkson in Spanish.

Clarkson grunted, then gave Graham a shove. *"Dónde está Esteban?"*

The guard nodded toward the elevator. *"Arriba."* Upstairs.

Another guard lay dead on the floor, which explained how Esteban and his men had gotten control of the building. Graham glanced away as Clarkson gave him another shove toward the elevator. They rode up in silence to the eighty-fifth floor where they were met by more of Esteban's armed men.

Graham was taken into a luxurious conference room where Esteban sat at the head of a gleaming ebony table. Another man confiscated the blueprints and handed them to Esteban.

"Welcome, Mr. Hollister. I've been waiting for you. Please…" Esteban nodded to the chair next to him. "Have a seat."

"I'd rather stand."

Esteban shrugged. "Suit yourself." He waved a hand toward the blueprints he'd placed on the table. "As you can see, we have a lot to go over."

"You've got the money," Graham said. "Seven million dollars. Let my wife go."

"I'm afraid I can't do that. Not yet at least."

"Why not? What more do you want from me?"

Esteban's dark eyes gleamed. "Tell me something, Mr. Hollister. If you wanted to inflict damage to this building, how would you go about it?"

Fear churned in Graham's stomach. "What do you mean?"

"You designed the PemCo Tower. You must know its weaknesses better than anyone."

"You're out of your mind if you think I'll help you."

Esteban just laughed. "We'll see about that."

He flicked his wrist, and one of his men sat down at the table and opened a laptop. With a few keystrokes, he located a Web site and waited for it to load. Then he muttered to himself and typed a few more keys. After a moment he looked up.

"The woman. She is gone." He looked terrified when he said it.

Esteban sat rigid for a moment, and then slowly he turned, his eyes burning with cold rage.

Graham smiled. "She's somewhere safe," he said. "Someplace where you'll never find her."

Esteban rose, trembling with rage. "Kill him!" he screamed.

But before his men could draw their weapons, Clarkson and his associate whipped off their masks and started firing.

It all happened so fast then that Graham had no time to process his fear. He dived for cover as bullets whizzed over his head.

He saw Esteban disappear through a door at the back of the conference room, and, keeping low, Graham rushed after him. He could hear the gun battle raging fiercely behind him as he raced into the hallway. A door up ahead swished closed, and Graham lunged toward it, pausing briefly inside to get his bearings. A set of stairs led up to the observation deck on the roof. If Esteban had gone up there, he was trapped. Graham had him.

Drawing the weapon that Clarkson had given him earlier, Graham ran up the stairs. He eased the door open and stepped out on the roof, his gaze quickly scanning his surroundings.

The moment he stepped onto the roof, Graham could feel the vertigo pulling at his balance. He stumbled, and his loss of balance saved him. A bullet sang passed his cheek, and Graham hit the deck. He saw Esteban then, a dark shadow racing toward the elevator in the far wall.

"Stop!"

Esteban whirled and fired.

Graham tried to focus. Tried to gain control of the panic that siezed him as the building spun beneath him. Blinking away the sweat that dripped into his eyes, he drew a bead on Esteban and squeezed the trigger. The bullet hit him in the shoulder and the gun slid from his grip.

One hand clutching the bullet wound, he watched as Graham rose and walked toward him. "Kick the gun over here," he said.

Esteban laughed. "Getting off a lucky shot in the heat of the moment is very different from killing a man in cold blood. You don't have it in you, *mi amigo*."

"You're wrong," Graham said, and fired again.

"Mr. Kittering?"

Leo had been standing at the window in his office, gazing out into the courtyard, his mind a million miles away. He wanted to lash out at the unwelcome visitor, but instead he turned, his brows lifting in surprise when he saw who it was.

"Maria!" he said in delight. "What brings you here this time of night?"

"I have a message from Hector." The young woman stood in the doorway, and even from across the room, Leo could see tears glistening on her cheeks.

"What is it?" he said in consternation. Surely nothing had gone wrong in Houston. Hector would have called Leo himself. He wouldn't have sent his sister with a message of any import.

"My brother has been arrested," she said. "He's in an American jail."

The pulse in Leo's neck jumped erratically. "How do you know this?"

"I heard from him myself. He said to tell you that Esteban and his men are dead and the woman is gone."

"Gone?" Leo stared at her as if she'd taken leave of her senses. "That's impossible. My men are guarding her. No one can get to her."

"Your men are all dead. Hector said to tell you that it's all over." Maria turned to walk away, but Leo stopped her.

"Where are you going?"

"It's not safe here," she said, and for a moment, Leo could have sworn he saw pity in her eyes. "They're coming for you, too."

For the first time in a very long time, Leo Kittering felt real fear. "Who?"

She turned and disappeared down the hallway without another word.

Before she reached the stairs, though, Maria turned and glanced over her shoulder. The gunshot that came from Leo's office brought a knowing smile to her lips.

Chapter Fourteen

Awakened by the quickly descending Cessna, Graham sat up and rubbed his eyes.

He wouldn't have imagined that he would be able to sleep on the flight down from Houston. Only forty-eight hours ago, he'd shot a man. Taken another life without hesitation, and yet he'd drifted off the moment the plane left the tarmac.

It was the first real rest he'd had in days, even after Esteban had been eliminated and he knew Kendall was tucked away in one of Clarkson's safe-houses. Clearing his name with the FBI had been no small feat, but Terrence hadn't been kidding when he said Nathan Clarkson had connections. With Esteban and his men dead and Hector Reyes all too willing too cooperate, the truth had finally been sorted out.

But that was only the beginning. Graham had had to come to terms with a very harsh reality— the woman he'd been living with for the past five years wasn't his wife. The contents of Nikki Singer's safety deposit box had confirmed Clarkson's suspicions.

As if reading Graham's mind, Clarkson leaned back from the copilot's seat as the Cessna touched down. "You okay?"

"I will be."

"You sure you're ready to face her?"

Graham shrugged, but didn't answer.

SO IT HAD come to this, Nikki thought as she walked barefoot in the surf, waiting for a phone call she feared would never come. Graham knew who she was. He knew *where* she was. And he'd chosen not to come for her.

She didn't blame him, of course. She should have told him the truth a long time ago. She should have trusted in their love, and now it was too late. He would never be able to forgive her.

She shivered and pulled the shawl tightly around her shoulders. Now that the sun had gone down, the breeze from the water was chilly, but she couldn't make herself go inside. The house was comfortable, but that didn't stop the walls from closing in on her. That didn't stop the regret from eating her up inside.

"Kendall?"

She whirled. And her heart stopped.

There he was. The man she thought of as her

husband. The man she had once planned to spend the rest of her life with.

The man she had lied to and deceived. The man whose wife had died and he had not been allowed to grieve. Because of her.

"I guess I should call you Nikki."

She tightened the shawl around her shoulders, unable to utter a word. Tears threatened behind her lids and she turned to stare out at the water.

"I didn't think you'd come," she finally said.

"I wasn't sure I wanted to," he admitted. "I guess I just needed to hear your side of it."

She nodded and tried to swallow past the knot in her throat.

"Why did you do it?" he asked.

She drew another breath. "I was scared and in trouble. You were my only way out."

"You killed L. J. Kittering, didn't you?"

She nodded.

"What happened?"

She hesitated. "It's getting cold out here. Let's go back to the house. I'll tell you everything you want to know."

They walked back in silence, and it seemed to Nikki that Graham was careful to keep enough distance between them so that there would be no accidental contact. When she glanced at him, he wouldn't even look at her.

She rubbed the back of her hand across her face.

How was she going to fix this? How could she possibly make things right? Even if she could somehow make him understand, he would never be able to forgive her. He would never trust her again. And she had no one to blame but herself.

She opened the door of the bungalow and he followed her inside. She turned on a lamp and the soft light cast shadows over his face as he stood looking around.

His appearance stunned her. His eyes were bloodshot and he hadn't shaved in days. He looked exhausted and worn out, but not worn down. There was something oddly feral about the way he took a quick assessment of his surroundings.

Leo Kittering had been right, she thought in despair. Whatever Graham had done to get her back had changed him. The man she'd known was gone forever.

His hard gaze met hers and she shivered.

"Were you in love with Kittering?"

The question shocked her. "No! I despised him."

Something flickered in Graham's eyes. "Why did you leave your job at the consulate to work for Leo Kittering?"

"Because I wanted to make L.J. pay for what he'd done to my sister."

"Your sister?"

"She met L.J. on spring break one year. She was just a kid, and he was rich, handsome, sophisticated. He swept her off her feet. When everyone else went back to school after that week, she stayed behind to be with him. She even called and told me that he wanted to marry her. She was ecstatic. I'd never seen her like that. We had a pretty miserable childhood… an alcoholic mother, an abusive stepfather. I'll spare you the details. I was just so happy that she'd finally found the kind of love she deserved.

"But after a while, things changed. L.J. tired of her, and when she finally showed up back home, I hardly recognized her. He'd beaten her down, gotten her hooked on drugs and then he'd kicked her out. A few months after she came back home, she overdosed on heroin. I found her on the bathroom floor one night with the needle still in her arm."

Graham's gaze was still on her, but he didn't say a word. Nikki didn't know whether to take that as a good sign or not.

"I decided I was going to make him pay for what he'd done to my sister. I didn't know how or when, but I knew that I couldn't let him get away with it. I couldn't let him do to anyone else what he'd done to Melanie. And maybe a part of me wanted a reason to get away from my own crappy life. So I moved to Mexico, got a job with the consulate and started showing up at the places he liked to hang out. We had a lot of mutual acquaintances and I eventually landed a job with his father. That's where I met Kendall."

Graham stiffened and glanced away.

"We became friends, mostly because of our backgrounds, I suppose. We were both American, both single, both seemed to have a lot of skeletons in our closet. She told me about you." His back was still to Nikki and she hesitated. "I couldn't imagine even then why she'd look twice at someone like L. J. Kittering when she had you back home."

He said over his shoulder, "Don't."

"But it's true." She tucked a strand of hair behind one ear with a trembling hand. "What we had was real. I never lied about my feelings for you."

"What happened with Kittering?" he said without emotion.

"He beat her, too. I saw her with black eyes on two different occasions, but when I pressed her for the truth, she always protected him. Just like Melanie did. Then one night Kendall showed up at my apartment. She had more than a black eye that time. He'd really worked her over, nearly killed her. I tried to get her to go to the hospital, but she didn't want to. She said she had to get out of the country because she was afraid he was going to come find her and finish the job. She had her passport, some money, and she wanted me to drive her across the border.

"But before we could leave, L.J. showed up. He'd followed her to my apartment. He was drunk and in a rage, and I thought he was going to kill us both. I grabbed a knife from the kitchen, told him to leave,

but he wouldn't. He just kept coming at me until..."
She trailed off and drew a shaky breath. "I killed him."

Graham turned. "And then you ran."

She nodded. "I was in shock and I panicked. I knew what Leo would do if he found out. So I got Kendall out of the apartment and into her car. I think I had some vague notion of driving us both across the border. Except I didn't have my passport. No identification of any kind. Kendall's passport was found on the side of the cliff only a few feet from where I went through the windshield."

"Were you forced off the road?"

She shook her head. "No. The accident was all my fault. I was driving too fast and I lost control of the car. It went over the cliff and exploded on impact. The bottom of the cliff was at least a hundred feet down and nearly impossible to get to. So once they found the passport, they assumed I was Kendall Hollister, and that I'd been alone in the car."

"And you let everyone, including me, believe it."

"Because I knew that L.J.'s body must have been found in my apartment by then. And it was only a matter of time before Leo came after me."

"When I brought you back to the States...why didn't you tell me the truth then? I could have protected you."

"I wanted to," she said. "More than anything. I kept telling myself that once I knew I was safe, I would tell you everything. I kept putting it off because I was in love with you. And then you fell in love with me and I couldn't walk away from that. No one had ever loved me the way you did. It was the first time in my life I'd ever been truly happy. I didn't want to lose it. I didn't want to lose you."

"But it was all based on a lie," he said. "It wasn't real."

"It wasn't a lie. Nothing about us was a lie. Graham, you have to believe that. If nothing else, you have to believe what I felt for you—and what you felt for me—was real. Why does anything else have to matter?"

He shook his head sadly. "I don't know. But it does matter. And I can't help that."

"I know."

He glanced around aimlessly, as if unsure what he should do next. "What about Michael? Did he know who you were?"

"He figured it out. He and Kendall had been… close. I had no idea because she never talked about him. When I didn't respond to him the way he thought I should, he eventually put two and two together."

"The FBI thinks he's the one who told Kittering about you."

"I think so, too. I don't know how else he could have found out. But I don't suppose it matters anymore. Maybe he thought he was doing you a favor by getting rid of me."

"Somehow I don't think his motives were quite so altruistic," Graham said bitterly.

Nikki sighed. "No, probably not." She bit her lip. "So where do we go from here?"

"I'm flying back to Austin tonight," Graham said. "Clarkson has arranged for you to have this place for a few more days. That'll give me time to find an apartment. When you get back, you can stay on in the house until you decide what you want to do."

"So this is it, then?" For the first time, Nikki felt a surge of anger. "You're just going to walk away from what we had?"

"We didn't have anything. I was married to Kendall. You and I…"

"What?" Nikki prompted.

"Look." He ran a hand through his hair and glanced away. "I came down here to say goodbye. Let's not drag it out any longer than necessary."

"If that's the way you want it." She folded her arms and lifted her chin, but she could feel her lips tremble. "Goodbye, Graham."

HE WAS halfway back to the airport when the full impact of what he'd done struck him. He'd just said goodbye to the only woman he'd ever loved.

Kendall had been his legal wife, but she'd never loved him the way Nikki had. She would never have been content with the life the two of them had shared these past five years.

Graham had been to hell and back these past few days, and if he'd learned anything, it was that happiness could be snatched away in the blink of an eye. So why was he throwing it away so willingly?

Before he could change his mind, he turned the Jeep around and headed back to the beach house. When Nikki drew open the door, she stared at him for a moment, her eyes wary and sad and yet somehow hopeful.

He took a step toward her. "I don't know if this is going to work. I don't know anything except...I don't want to leave without you."

Her face crumpled. She put a hand to her mouth. "Are you sure?"

He closed his eyes briefly. "Just answer one question."

"Anything," she breathed.

"Do you love me?"

"More than anything. More than life itself."

"Then come home with me."

She lifted his hand to her scarred face and nodded. "There's nowhere in the world I'd rather be."

* * * * *

Available March 2008
THE DEVIL'S FOOTPRINTS
by
Amanda Stevens
from MIRA Books

The legend.

On the night of January 10, 1922, a full moon rose over the frozen countryside near Adamant, Arkansas, a tiny community five miles north of the Louisiana state line. The pale light glinted on freshly fallen snow and spotlighted the oil derrick recently constructed in Thomas Duncan's barren cotton field.

Despite the gusher that had been discovered on his property a few months after the Busey Number One had come in near El Dorado, Thomas refused to move to more comfortable accommodations in town, preferring instead to remain on the family farm he'd inherited from his father nearly half a century earlier.

Thomas liked being in the country. His nearest neighbor was nearly two miles away and he did sometimes get lonely, but the farm made him feel closer to his wife, Mary, who had passed away five years ago. She'd been laid to rest beneath a stand of cottonwoods on a hillock overlooking the river, and Thomas had tied bells in the branches so that she would have music whenever a breeze stirred.

All day long the chime of the bells had been lost in the icy howl of an arctic cold front that roared down from the northeast. The gusts had finally abated in the late afternoon, but the weather was still bitter, even for January and a snowfall—the first Thomas could remember in over a decade—blanketed his yard and fields in a wintry mantle. He watched the swirl of flakes from his front room window until dusk. Inexplicably uneasy, he fixed an early supper and went up to bed.

Something awakened him around midnight. The snowfall had brought a preternatural quiet to the countryside, the silence so profound that Thomas could easily discern the pump out in the field as it siphoned oil from deep within the earth. Early on, the mechanical rhythm had kept him awake until all hours, but he was used to it now and that wasn't what had disturbed his rest.

Still half-asleep, he thought at first he'd heard a gunshot and he wondered if someone was out tracking a deer through the snow. Then he worried there might have been an explosion at the well and he got up to glance out the window where the wooden derrick rose like an inky shadow from the pristine layer of snow.

As he crawled back under the warm covers, he heard the sound again, a loud, steady clank, like something being thrown against the tin roof of his house.

Or like heavy footsteps.

The hair on the back of Thomas's neck lifted as a terrible dread gripped him. He scrambled out of bed, pulled on his clothes and grabbed a shotgun and coat on his way outside.

Using a side door to avoid the slippery porch, he trudged around to the front of the house, where he had a better view of the roof.

The moon was bright on the snow, a luminous glow that turned nighttime into a subdued twilight, and the air was pure and so cold that his nostrils stung when he breathed. He turned, looked up and what he saw chilled him to the bone. Cloven hoofprints started at the edge of the roof, moved in a straight line up the sloping tin and disappeared over the peak.

Slowly Thomas turned in a circle, his gaze encompassing the yard, the barn, the cotton fields and finally his house again and up the porch steps right to his front door. He saw now what he had not noticed before. The footprints were everywhere. He'd never seen anything like them. He'd lived in the country all his life and he knew the tracks hadn't been made by a four-legged animal, but by something that walked upright. And the stride was long, at least twice as wide as the footprints Thomas had left in the snow.

A terrible premonition settled over him. The farmhouse had been his home since he was a boy, and on Sunday mornings when his neighbors headed into town for church services, he had instead walked the fields alone. The peace he found there was deep and profound, the clean silence of the freshly plowed earth more suited to his idea of prayer and reflection. But now as he stood in his own front yard, Thomas Duncan had the sense that a sacred place had been desecrated.

An urgency he couldn't explain prodded him, and he rushed back to the house, avoiding the prints on the steps and across the frozen porch as he flung open the front door. His heart hammered against his chest as he stepped inside, expecting to see melting tracks on the plank flooring. The only snow, however, was from his own boots.

Quickly he bolted the door and strode down the narrow hallway to the kitchen. As he opened the back door, his gaze dropped. The prints started at the threshold and continued down the steps and across the yard to the open field, as if something had come in the front door, passed through the house without making a sound or leaving a mark, and let itself out the back way.

More afraid than he'd ever been in his life, Thomas moved back inside and clicked the thumbblock on the door. He shoved a chair under the knob and sat down at the table, shotgun across his knees, to wait for daylight.

By morning, word of the footprints had spread through the town, and with it, speculation as to their source. One of Thomas's neighbors followed the tracks right up to the edge of the river, where they continued in the same straight line on the other side.

For several nights after that, some of the men sat up with Thomas, waiting to see if the strange phenomenon reoccurred. When nothing happened, the community began to breathe a little more easily until a local preacher sermonized that the drillers, in their quest to strike it rich, had somehow punched a hole straight down to hell, unleashing the devil himself to run unbridled across the countryside.

The cloven hoofprints vanished with the melting snow and were eventually forgotten in the tiny Arkansas community...until seven decades later when they reappeared near the mutilated body of sixteen-year-old Rachel DeLaune.

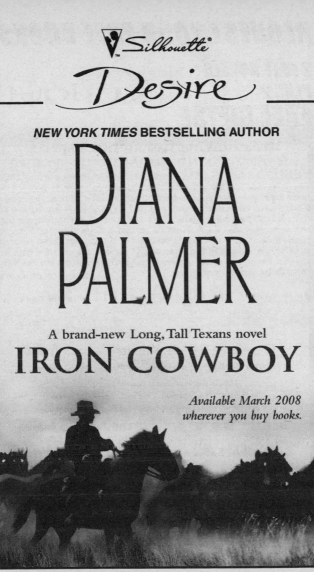

Silhouette®

Desire

NEW YORK TIMES BESTSELLING AUTHOR

DIANA PALMER

A brand-new Long, Tall Texans novel

IRON COWBOY

*Available March 2008
wherever you buy books.*

REQUEST YOUR FREE BOOKS!

2 FREE NOVELS PLUS 2 FREE GIFTS!

HARLEQUIN®

INTRIGUE®

Breathtaking Romantic Suspense

YES! Please send me 2 FREE Harlequin Intrigue® novels and my 2 FREE gifts. After receiving them, if I don't wish to receive any more books, I can return the shipping statement marked "cancel." If I don't cancel, I will receive 6 brand-new novels every month and be billed just $4.24 per book in the U.S., or $4.99 per book in Canada, plus 25¢ shipping and handling per book and applicable taxes, if any*. That's a savings of close to 15% off the cover price! I understand that accepting the 2 free books and gifts places me under no obligation to buy anything. I can always return a shipment and cancel at any time. Even if I never buy another book from Harlequin, the two free books and gifts are mine to keep forever.

182 HDN EEZ7   382 HDN EEZK

Name	(PLEASE PRINT)	
Address		Apt. #
City	State/Prov.	Zip/Postal Code
Signature (if under 18, a parent or guardian must sign)		

Mail to the Harlequin Reader Service®:
IN U.S.A.: P.O. Box 1867, Buffalo, NY 14240-1867
IN CANADA: P.O. Box 609, Fort Erie, Ontario L2A 5X3

Not valid to current Harlequin Intrigue subscribers.

Want to try two free books from another line?
Call 1-800-873-8635 or visit www.morefreebooks.com.

* Terms and prices subject to change without notice. NY residents add applicable sales tax. Canadian residents will be charged applicable provincial taxes and GST. This offer is limited to one order per household. All orders subject to approval. Credit or debit balances in a customer's account(s) may be offset by any other outstanding balance owed by or to the customer. Please allow 4 to 6 weeks for delivery.

Your Privacy: Harlequin is committed to protecting your privacy. Our Privacy Policy is available online at www.eHarlequin.com or upon request from the Reader Service. From time to time we make our lists of customers available to reputable firms who may have a product or service of interest to you. If you would prefer we not share your name and address, please check here. ☐

HI07

the DEVIL'S footprints

**Don't miss
the latest thriller from**

AMANDA STEVENS

On sale March 2008!

AMANDA STEVENS

the DEVIL'S footprints

MARKED BY EVIL.